GOLD MAN REVIEW

ISSUE 15

Gold Man Review is published annually by Gold Man Publishing.

The editors invite submissions of previously unpublished works of fiction, nonfiction, and poetry. Manuscripts can be submitted at www.goldmanpublishing.com by following our submission guidelines.

Address all requests to:
Heather Cuthbertson
Editor-in-Chief
Heather.Cuthbertson@GoldManPublishing.com

Contents

Issue 15 Editor's Letter   vii

FICTION

The Interpreter's Daughter   3
elina kumra

Taxi   8
cecilia januszewski

Salty Cans & Rusty Sunglasses   21
nicholas viglietti

Caliguluck   24
laine perry

Darkling   31
evan morgan williams

Baby Girl   46
lenore weiss

POETRY

Ode to a Book in the Ten Dollar
All You Can Bag Book Sale
merridawn duckler
51

Scramble
shobha tharoor srinivasan
52

My Soul is in the Bottom Drawer
ian day
53

Hierarchy
joanna scandiffio
54

Komorebi
alexandra bergmann
55

Pacific Ocean
joshua kepfer
56

NONFICTION

Leonard Cohen Hated Me (Maybe Not)   59
lance mazmania

I Don't Know How to Pronounce Bolognese   63
bee lazar

A Tale of Two Mothers   66
kristy webster

Petrified Dog Shit   81
julia medina

Issue 15 Contributors   89

Issue 15 Editor's Letter

It's our decade-and-a-half birthday here at *Gold Man Review*! It's been a long road figuring out how to build a journal that stands out in a sea of others, but I think we're finally coming into our own. Publishing our fifteenth issue feels huge. The number fifteen is all about manifestation and positive change—and honestly, that feels right for where *Gold Man* is headed.

Every October, when I sit down to write this letter, I end up looking back on the past year. Most people probably do that around New Year's, but for me, it's become my own version of a check-in—time to think about what I've learned, how my writing has grown, and where I still want to go. This past year has been a rollercoaster when it comes to publishing, but I've made it through stronger and clearer about what I want—and what I don't.

For a long time, I had this picture in my head of what getting a publishing deal would look like. When it finally happened, that picture cracked. But like the stories in Issue 15, it needed to. Those cracks opened up space for something better—new ways of seeing, writing, and understanding what this literary life really means.

This issue reminds me that literature's power doesn't come from neat resolutions—it comes from the breaks, the questions that don't get answered. From the interpreter who chooses comfort over honesty, the beachside friends who learn that even rust can shine, and the daughter who faces the truth no one wants to say out loud. The poems, too, find beauty in unexpected places—like Merridawn Duckler's ode to the small miracles hiding inside a ten-dollar bag of books. And our nonfiction digs into what it means to tell your own story, from Bee Lazar's funny, tender take on language and belonging to the quiet truths that surface across these essays. Together, they remind us that words can hurt and heal at the same time—and sometimes they guide us exactly where we didn't know we needed to go.

At *Gold Man Review*, we've always been drawn to work that unsettles, that lingers long after you finish reading. Issue 15 keeps that spirit alive: fiction that explores the messy middle of love and loss, nonfiction that finds humor even in grief, and poetry that turns the ordinary into something luminous. In a lot of ways, this issue feels like a reflection of who we've become as a journal—braver, more honest, and more willing to live in the in-between.

To the writers: thank you for trusting us with your words.

To the readers: thank you for showing up, for sitting with these stories and letting them stay with you. My hope is that somewhere in these pages, you'll find something that feels familiar, something that reminds you of yourself.

With gratitude,

Heather Cuthbertson
Editor-in-Chief
Gold Man Review

Gold Man Review Editors
Issue 15

FICTION

The Interpreter's Daughter

elina kumra

The hospital translator's badge says MARIE CHEN but I haven't answered to that name since the miscarriage. In Mandarin, my mother calls me 晚晴—evening clear after rain—though I was born at noon in a drought year. "Anticipatory naming," she explained once. "We name toward what we lack."

Today's assignment: oncology ward, Vietnamese grandmother, brain tumor pressing on the speech center. The family clusters—three daughters, one son, nine grandchildren wearing Minecraft t-shirts and worry. The eldest daughter grips my wrist: "She keeps saying 'con chim.' Bird? Is she saying bird?"

The grandmother's eyes track something invisible near the ceiling. *"Con chim đã về,"* she whispers. The birds have returned home.

I translate: "She's comfortable. The medication is working."

My mother's stroke came during The View, her afternoon talk show. I found her at 4:17 PM, still clutching the remote, the anchors arguing about cancel culture while she lay folded into the couch like a pressed flower. Her left side: a country that had declared independence.

The paramedics asked questions. I translated her silence into medical history.

"Why you lie?" my mother managed three weeks later, in the rehab center. Half her face still on strike, but her fury intact.

"About what?"

"Con chim." She'd heard. Somehow, through the hospital's Vietnamese networks, she'd heard about the grandmother and the birds. "You know what it means."

What con chim means: the soul preparing for flight. What I told the family: clinical comfort. The difference: hope's last thread, severed clean.

"Better that way," I said.

My mother's good hand found her teacup, gripped it like a throat. "教你残忍?" Who taught you such cruelty?

The answer lived in this room seventeen years ago. Me, interpreting at my father's ICU bedside. The doctor's percentages became my promises. My mother nodded, planned his homecoming meal—fish for luck, noodles for long life. Six hours later: the fish uneaten, the noodles uncooked, my translation revealed as fiction.

She didn't speak to me for a month.

The Vietnamese grandmother dies on a Tuesday. Her eldest daughter sends me a card: "Thank you for making her last words peaceful."

I don't correct the record. Some lies calcify into kindness.

My mother's physical therapy: Tuesdays and Thursdays, 3 PM. She insists on taxi fare, refuses my car. "I need practice," she says, though we both know it's punishment. I watch from the parking lot as she counts exact change with her good hand, the driver impatient, her left arm cradled against her chest.

When I was nine, my mother taught me to fold paper cranes. "One thousand and your wish comes true." We made it to 987 before my father's diagnosis. The remaining thirteen blank papers still live in her sewing box.

Now she folds hospital brochures one-handed into lopsided birds. "For practice," she says. They accumulate on her nightstand, a flock of broken-winged insurance policies.

"新病房的越南人." Another Vietnamese, my supervisor texts. "Terminal. Family requesting you specifically."

I forward the request to Michael, the other translator. White guy, learned Vietnamese in the Peace Corps, pronounces tones like a xylophone. But clinically accurate. No birds in his vocabulary.

"You sure?" he asks.

"I'm sure."

My mother calls at midnight. Since the stroke, she keeps vampire hours. "I dream in English now," she says. "What does that mean?"

"It means you're tired."

"No. It means I'm losing."

"Losing what?"

"家." Home. But she says it in English, which proves her point.

Her next appointment, I arrive early. She's in the lobby, teaching origami to a child with a cochlear implant. The bird emerges from her good hand, precise. The child signs something. My mother signs back, fluid.

"When did you learn ASL?"

"YouTube," she says. "When you can't speak, you find other ways."

The child's bird is crumpled, eager. My mother adjusts one wing with her teeth.

Late shift at the hospital. A Mandarin-speaking woman, my age, positive pregnancy test after five years of IVF. She grips her husband's hand while I explain beta levels, cautious optimism. In the middle of translating "viable pregnancy," I taste copper—blood memory from my own loss.

"你确定?" Are you certain? she asks.

I look at her chart, the numbers. "Yes. Congratulations."

In Mandarin, she tells her husband they'll name the baby after birds—燕子 for a girl, swallow. 鹰 for a boy, eagle. "So, they can fly far from suffering."

I dream of con chim. They speak all languages, carry messages between the living and the leaving. My father rides one, young again, his hospital gown transformed into feathers.

"Tell your mother—" he begins.

I wake before the translation.

My mother's final rehab evaluation. The occupational therapist, kind Midwestern vowels, asks about goals. My mother demonstrates her chopstick grip, improved range of motion. Then, in careful English: "I want to translate. Like my daughter. But honest."

The OT looks at me, confused. I translate nothing.

Two months later: St. Mary's Hospice Center needs Mandarin/Cantonese interpreter. Mom applies with her good hand, types résumé hunt-and-peck. Lists me as reference.

"You can't—" I start.

"Cannot what? Tell dying people truth? I practice whole life for this job."

They hire her. Part-time, as needed. She carries a pocket dictionary and her folder of paper birds. When families ask about final words, she gives them origami. "Your loved one's spirit," she says, "folded into wings."

We develop a system. She handles the dying; I handle the living. Sometimes our shifts overlap—me in maternity, her in hospice, the hospital a way station between arrivals and departures.

One Thursday, we meet in the cafeteria. She's folding the daily menu into something elaborate.

"What's that one?"

"Phoenix," she says. "看." Look.

The bird is intricate, impossible. Her weak hand holds while her strong hand creates. When finished, it balances on one wing tip, perpetually almost falling.

"For the Vietnamese family," she says. "The grand-mother's daughter, she comes back. Wants to know real last words."

"What will you tell her?"

"Truth. But with wings."

She places the phoenix in her bag, between dictionar-ies. Her left-hand trembles against the table—tiny earth-quakes, aftershocks of the stroke. I cover it with mine.

"妈—"

"I know," she says in English. Then, in Mandarin: "我们都是候鸟." We are all migratory birds.

"Going where?"

She points with her good hand—up, through the hospi-tal ceiling, past the floors of birth and death, toward what-ever sky waits beyond the fluorescent lights.

"Home," she says. "Eventually, all birds go home."

The shift ends. We walk to the parking lot together, her leaning slightly left, me carrying both our bags. The au-tomatic doors part. Outside, evening birds lift from the power lines. They rise together against the dimming sky.

"Con chim," my mother says, watching them disappear.

This time, I don't correct her pronunciation. Some truths survive any language. Some flights require no translation.

Taxi

cecilia januszewski

I used to live in Alaska. Not for very long, just a couple months the year after I graduated college, but long enough. When I think of it now, I think of pine, and the long dark sky, and the sweet, dangerous smell of rotting crustaceans.

One guy in town used to disappear for weeks, then return wiry and wind-whipped to sell crab out of the back of his pickup truck. I bought from him a few times. His prices weren't really much better than the grocery store, but it was fresh-fresh. Right out of the water fresh. Fresh like I would never be able to find again, ever, once I left the state. Fresh.

There wasn't much to do in Alaska, so he and I got to be good friends. Malone, square and tall and bearded, selling his crab out of the post office parking lot, and me, short and fat, hair tucked into my crocheted hat and still shivering. It wasn't even that cold, but the hard wind off the sea made it so that no amount of layers could keep me warm.

Malone was friendly in the weird way that everyone in town was. West Coast smiley but too used to being alone to act normally when you spoke to him. He was a nice guy who looked at you for too long without blinking, so I preferred to sit beside him in the truck bed rather than standing to face him. That way we didn't have to look at anything but the water.

I was lonely there, which is why I was willing to talk to him in the first place. Anywhere else I would have sped up and walked past a stony-eyed stranger selling seafood out of his car, but there, where my options were limited to him, my sullen, stoner roommate, or the kid in the library whose anxiety prevented him from forming words in my presence, I didn't have much choice.

One day, I asked Malone to drive me to the grocery store, which was several miles of empty road away. It was rural enough there that most people had multiple jobs to keep the town running. Malone sold crabs, mostly, but he was also the taxi when somebody needed it. On that day he'd said he had a stop to make before dropping me in town, but I could come if I wanted. I accepted. There was nowhere else I had to be.

Malone's truck was from the eighties, white with red leather seats and peeling paneling. It rattled and stank, and he was pretty much in love with it. He'd given it a name, which I don't recall now, and every time he referred to her, he slapped her flank the way you might do with a large dog or a horse.

Before arriving in Alaska, I had never understood why people named their cars. Or their trucks, sorry. Malone explained to me that those were different things. Boats I could understand, out in that big gray waiting, I'd want someone to talk to too. When you're out against the ocean, you want someone on your side, even if that someone turns out to be a boat you've named after your great aunt Lizzie. Cars, though? Trucks? For me, for a long time, they were nothing more than a way to get from A to B.

In that town in that state, though, I could understand a little better. With the great unnamed mountains biting into the sky all around you and the pine trees thick with ravens, driving into the woods really did seem like we were heading into an ocean. It was just Malone and I, and the gaudy old truck, facing down an unpaved road that led into a dark forest hundreds of miles long and dozens of stories deep.

Malone turned on the radio without saying anything, and we listened to some guy singing a folk song before he turned it off again. We drove twenty miles without speaking. That was another thing I'd noticed about that town: sometimes people spoke like they were afraid they never would again, and other times they had nothing to say and didn't particularly care to hear from you either.

I stared at tree trunks. There wasn't anything else to look at. After a while I remembered to ask where we were going.

"Probably should have asked that earlier," I joked. "Make sure you weren't trying to kidnap me."

Malone looked at me out of the corner of his eye. "No," he said. We hit a bump, and the crates of crab in the back rattled. I wanted to get out. Being in Alaska, though, I was probably safer with him than alone in the mountains. We'd gone too far from the town for me to be able to get back by myself, and I knew that the forest would be dark as soon as his headlights faded into the distance. That's assuming he would even be willing to leave me alone.

For the most part, people from that town were pretty live-and-let-live, but they knew me and knew what to protect me from. My first week there I had tried to go on a solo hike to see the sunset, and somehow about half of the town found out about it and tried to dissuade me. There would be bears, they said. There already were, but they especially liked to come out at that time of day. And did I have emergency rations? A flashlight? Was I wearing layers and did I have extra water? Bear bells? I had not known that I would need those things, and before I could protest, they had guided me to the tavern, the only one in town, so they could keep an eye on me until the light ran out. My indifference, they had warned me, would prove fatal if I entertained it for long enough. Self-preservation would have to kick in at some point, and if it didn't come naturally to me, I'd have to decide to make it happen. Otherwise, they'd warned, as good naturedly as possible, considering the fact that we were discussing my imminent death, I would never leave.

There had been several instances like that, where I, unaware of the danger bordering the town, had tried to venture out on my own and been cajoled back. It annoyed me, but I was grateful. I would have been dead many times over if they hadn't.

Malone looked like he could tell what I was thinking and slapped the side of the truck. "She'll keep us safe," he said. "Hasn't broken down yet."

"Don't say that, you'll jinx us."

"Nah. She's good luck." He eyed me. "*You* might jinx us though."

"Why me? I know not to go poking at fur traps now. Maybe you're the jinx."

"You poked at a trap? Jesus."

I slouched down in my seat. "I didn't know what it was until Ted started yelling." Ted was my neighbor, who had offered to show me the trail in his backyard and now wouldn't let me on his property for fear I would get a limb severed by one of his traps.

It was silent again, and the truck seemed to speed up. From the cracks between the branches, I could see the sky was darkening. Soon all that was visible was the stretch of dirt illuminated by the headlights and the bony branches that intruded on the road. They scraped the windows. I kept thinking I saw something lurking in the woods and couldn't tell if it was a moose or a bear.

After a while we turned onto a paved part of the road, which turned into a highway. We were driving along the coast, a part I didn't recognize. The water was silver and deep, and when I opened the window, it smelled like stone and frost and salt. Malone glanced sideways at me when I cranked the glass down, and I put it back up.

"Too cold for that," he grunted. He stared out at the road. The light of the moon reflecting off the sea was just enough to see by and washed everything in gray. Malone stared straight ahead, unblinking. I reached out to turn the radio on but could only find static.

"Know any songs?" he asked me, and I said I did. From there on we sang what we could remember of a couple old musicals, pop songs from the previous year, and whatever else we could remember. He didn't have a phone, at least not one that could play music, and I never got service outside the main street of the town anyway. He had an okay voice, one which could carry a tune but was thin, wandering in a way that made everything sound mournful.

"You can't really sing, can you?" he said suddenly. I closed my mouth. He started singing something from Les Mis as I stared out the window. "Come on," he said after a few seconds. "Don't leave me hanging."

"You just—"

"I said you can't sing, not don't sing." So, we sang. The time passed more quickly after that, and I didn't notice the scenery as much.

When we stopped it was dark and cold. We had been driving for hours, and one of my legs was asleep. Malone lit an electric lantern and perched it on the hood of the truck.

"Pit stop," he said. There was a pebbly beach a few feet from where we'd stopped, where the water frothed and hissed on the rocks. We sat down on a dried-out, skeletal log to look at it.

"You know I have work tomorrow," I said, but I was already starting to resign myself to missing it.

"Yup." He lit up, and we smoked in silence.

"What time is it?"

"Dunno." We looked out at the water. "Sometimes there's the Northern Lights here," he said, jutting his chin toward the sky. It stretched out blank and dark before us.

"Yeah? I guess not tonight."

The song he was humming caught on the wind and blew away before I could identify it, and he shook his head. The water slurped at our feet. I dipped a hand in then yanked it out. It was too cold to be playing around in ocean water. Malone dug around in the glove compartment and pulled out a pair of mittens for me. They were hand knitted, with a pattern of stars on them.

"You're the only person I know who actually keeps gloves in the glove compartment."

"Everyone here does."

I looked down at them, too large on my hands. "Huh."

He brought out a blanket and draped it over my shoulders and wrapped a scarf around himself. I could see his breath.

"So, where're we going?" I asked.

"Just driving, for now." He handed me the blunt, looked at me sideways. "It'll take a while."

"Okay."

"If you keep driving, you have to eventually hit the end. Of the road. The land."

"Unless you end up back where you started."

He gave me a long look and blew a cloud of smoke into my face. "Not me," he said. "I'll just keep on driving up into the sky."

I was starting to get stoned, and this seemed like a plausible plan. "But what are you gonna' do when you get there?"

"Shell crabs."

"That's it?"

"Yup."

This seemed so brilliantly, mundanely ridiculous that I began to laugh, and fell over twitching into the pebbles. Malone exhaled serenely, staring up at the sky.

"I'll go live there," he said, pointing to a cluster of stars. "Not too bright, but not too far off from the neighbors. Got a bunch of crabs in the back. I'll drive back down next season. Get some more."

"Oh. Well at least I'll get to see you when you come back. I'll miss you."

"No, you come with me. Look at all the space up there." He gestured upward, inarticulately. I thought about all the space between here and the town, and the distance between us and the stars seemed much shorter. It was cold, and I was tired.

"Sure."

He snuffed out the blunt before I could take it back and got up. He vanished into the dark and I heard a stream of liquid, the zip of his jeans, and then he was back.

"Go now," he said. "We might not stop for a while." So, I ventured out into the dark too, making sure not to lose sight of the lantern, and pulled down my pants. When I got back, I was shivering, and we got in the truck quickly and without discussion. My phone, when I tried to check it, had completely died. Malone didn't have a charger, and I shut it in the glove compartment. We sang a little, quieter now, slow songs that dissolved into humming when we forgot the words.

Day was breaking pink and clean across the horizon when we stopped again. My eyelids were puffy, and Malone had dark purple streaks under his eyes. We drank a couple of juice boxes he found in the backseat and broke into his emergency stash of dried salmon. I didn't feel any better after eating, and the headache that had been developing threatened to turn into a migraine. The weed had run out, and all our songs had been sung. I squinted into the sun and stretched my hip while Malone went for a brief walk, up the highway and back. There were no other cars in sight, he said, and I believed him. We hadn't passed anyone all night.

"There might be hunters though," he told me. "Don't go too far from here." I remembered with dread the cold teeth of Ted's trap, camouflaged with pine branches. As if he could hear me thinking, Malone shook his head. "Guns," he said, "Not traps."

That was worse. I stuck close to the truck.

We got back in and drove on, toward the sun. Daylight glazed the pavement, and I had to look away. Malone didn't, though. He just kept staring down the highway, not blinking.

"You're going to go blind."

He shook his head. "No, I won't."

He would, though. My mother was an optometrist. I knew these things. But Malone kept staring into the sun, until eventually it dawned on me that if he was hell bent on going blind, he shouldn't be the one driving. I nudged him.

"Hey, give me a turn. You should rest." But he wouldn't, he just kept staring at the sun and singing until I begged him to stop. My migraine had built up to the point where the white daylight and Malone's reedy voice were unbearable.

I needed to lay down, but he wasn't willing to stop. The next few hours were agonizing, pulsing, hallucinatory, which the loud coughs from the truck's old engine made worse. I finally fell asleep, kind of, enough to get some relief from it. I dreamed of being fired. The trail crew I worked for was composed mostly of people like me, in between jobs or having just graduated college, all of us broke and replaceable.

I woke up, checked my phone and remembered that it was dead. Malone had stopped humming.

"How close are we?"

He didn't really respond, just made a raspy gurgle from deep in his throat. I stared at him, and he did it again.

"Are you laughing?" The sound came again, and he grinned. He mouthed something, voiceless, but I couldn't read lips. "It was the goddamn singing, wasn't it? That I told you to stop? God."

He nodded. The car had been slowly drifting toward the wrong side of the road as we'd been speaking, but Malone did nothing to correct it. I let him keep drifting for a minute, then yanked the wheel toward me. He jolted and glowered in my direction.

"Pull over." His eyebrows sank low over his eyes, and he wouldn't look at me. "Pull over," I said again. "I'll follow whatever road you want, just let me do it."

Malone didn't answer. His eyes, I noticed now, had developed an unusual sheen. Milky blue and glistening, like precious stones. The shadows under his eyes were starting to look as if they'd take up his whole face, and his skin had turned a delicate shade of gray.

"Do you need to stop?" He shook his head vigorously.

"Liar." We both looked out at the empty highway. "Fine. I'll just pull the wheel if we're drifting, then. Thank god there's no one else on the road."

He looked satisfied with that, and we went on. The day passed. Then night. The end of the land came quickly upon us. It happened so quickly I almost didn't catch it, but all at once we were off the highway and heading through a dark wood. At first, I thought it was another pine forest, but there were no trees. There was nothing, nothing but blue dark and a chill that permeated the truck. There was no light behind us to indicate which direction we had come from, and nothing before us to show where to aim. I don't know how Malone managed to navigate it, or if there even was a path to follow. From what I could tell, one direction was the same as any other.

But he did manage, somehow. Like he'd known all along how to get there.

When we arrived it was like Alaska, only without crab and without trees. Or bear or moose or mountains. So not much like Alaska, but the feeling of peering out into the dense blue wild was the same. A great shining house passed us on the right side, then one on the left, then others grouped together. They were ramshackle, most of them, but lit from within, shining dappled silver and green with walls like abalone. We did not stop. Once we'd passed through the bright place they grew sparse again, until one only appeared every minute or so.

Malone turned and kept on in that direction until we reached one of the houses. It had a decaying porch and sagging roof and glimmered faintly in the dark. He turned the ignition off and went inside, but I stayed in the truck. He was gone for longer than I would have liked. Eventually I got out too, cautiously.

It was silent there. There seemed to be a strong wind, but it made no sound, just pushed through my hair and under my coat. It smelled heavy and vaguely sweet.

"Malone," I said, but could barely hear anything. I yelled, and he appeared in the window.

He cocked his head to one side.

"Hi," I said. "We made it."

He came outside and started unpacking the back of the truck. There were dozens of crabs there, their brittle limbs bright and tangled under the tarp. As he walked past me with the first load I coughed. It smelled of rot.

"Malone," I said, and reached for a crab. "These are bad. Like, really bad. You can't use these."

He ignored me. After depositing them in the house he came back and took another load. I leaned against the side of the truck and watched him trudging back and forth. After a while I got cold and sat in the truck, in the driver's seat, with the window down.

"So how long is this errand going to take? I'm kind of hungry." He gestured toward the crabs in the back, vehemently, still voiceless. "Do you want help? I can get them out and you bring them in?"

He nodded and patted me on the shoulder to say thanks, then picked up another bunch of crabs. Some of their legs fell off and disappeared, but the rotten smell stayed. I held my breath and shoved them out of the back, not paying any particular attention to keeping them intact.

It didn't take very long for me, but Malone was slower. The intervals between entering and emerging from the house began to grow longer and longer, and eventually he stopped coming back at all. I leaned against the truck and stared at the house. Its shine seemed to shift slightly depending on how you looked at it, but there was no external source of light to explain it. I amused myself looking at it for a while, then got antsy.

The front door was open, and the room inside was iridescent. Everything was. Malone was sitting at a circular table, shelling crabs.

"You know there's another load out there, right?"

His skin had acquired the same greenish opalescence that the house had, and when he nodded it was slow, as if underwater. The crab he was holding had gone blue and smelled unbearable, but he continued shelling it. Slowly.

"Please don't eat that," I said. "Even I can tell that's gone off." It smelled rank. I wanted to sneeze to get the scent out of my nose but couldn't.

He didn't eat it, but he also didn't answer.

"Alright, well. I have to get to town." I waited a second to see if he'd respond then, when he didn't, scooped the keys off the table and left.

There was no road to follow, but the trail of houses glowing in the dark led me back the way we'd come, through the village and back toward the forest on the other side. There was no light on the other end, so I drove the way Malone had, blindly. By the time I landed back on the highway it was dawn. Everything was flushed with sunrise, and a caravan of rusting trucks I passed flicked their lights at me in greeting.

I turned into the first town I passed. They had a charger and a cup of coffee, and the long-toothed woman who ran the cafe spent an hour lecturing me on crochet stitches when she'd noticed my threadbare hat. Even though I'd been offline for days, I didn't have that many messages. My boss had called twice, once to express concern, once to threaten to fire me. In the bathroom hallway, while tracing the knots in the wood paneling and drawing crabs in the dust on the picture frames, I called him back. I quit, I said, which was just as well. He'd been having doubts about me anyways, he told me.

When I eventually got back to town my housemate registered a kind of dull surprise that I was still alive, then profound revulsion at the rotten crab smell that was still clinging to my clothes. We had never been close, but my sudden pungent apparition and announcement that I was moving out turned our companionable silence into an icy one.

There were two flights out of Juneau the next day, and I booked the earlier one. I started to text Malone for a ride to the airport before realizing that I had his truck. There was no one else to take it, no family that I knew of to pass it off to. Standing outside, I toyed with the idea of taking over the taxi business. I had no other prospects, other than returning home to New England and seeing what kind of work I could scrounge up there. But I decided, inevitably, to go. I gave the truck an experimental slap, the way Malone did, just to see how it felt, and my hand, damp from showering, froze lightly onto the metal. I thought about his promise to return once his supply of crabs had run out, how I'd promised to see him again when he came back, and yanked my hand away. A thin film of skin stuck to the metal. Wincing, shivering, I went to find my suitcase.

Salty Cans & Rusty Sunglasses

nicholas viglietti

It was the law of the beach: all men turn to rust. No warning for when it hits. Reasons are vague in a transactional existence. All you can do is spend time and take it as a memory. The page flipping hours harden you and break you down like decorative furniture not far from the waves.

At least the view ain't bad. The sunlight in the alley looks better than it did in other cities I've lived in. Out on the boardwalk, different brands of swimwear move, North & South, like migrating birds, confused about which exhilarating direction to go.

I was barreling through my third year here and stiffly set, like yesterday's poured concrete, in the smooth rhythms of a salty tune. Good waves rolled in, and more beer was the only reason to leave the pleasure on the porch. Our hideout in plain sight, and endless smiles were an easy stroll away.

Elder Steve was our neighbor—E.S. as we called him—and across the narrow street from our porch, he resided. We were three bro-migos in our mid-twenties, and E.S. was maybe 35 to 40 years our senior. A relic in the area like a rust covered beach cruiser, locked up and forgotten.

He would go to the bar with us, but his liver didn't have our stamina. The right combination of chemicals could keep him up late, functioning at our pace, telling stories on the porch as the ocean's power pulsated a short distance away.

His youthful charisma reminded me of a boat that accumulates barnacles quickly, and yet, still makes passes on the bay. I could never tell whether it was age or money that supplied his confidence to chat up ladies decades his junior.

After another year, our routine was as consistent as the summer fun tourists that flood Mission Beach when the warm, seasonal change hits. I had a much-needed day off, so I went surfing with my roommate, bro-migos. Between wave sets, I mentioned, "Haven't seen E.S. last few days."

"He's probably visiting Hong Kong down in Mexico, and decided to extend the trip," Shanders hollered, taking off on a curling lip.

We rode through dead hours on Mother Earth's rolling energy and sent smiling praises to the big-braddah upstairs. After several swell servings, bellied up at the aqua-bar (ocean), we returned to the sun-soaked porch to sip a few south-of-the-border recovery beers.

My wide frame shades blocked the nuclear radiation from the sun, and my skin rusted from the rays. The ambulance arrived as groups of beach towels and coolers lumbered up our street to bake in the afternoon oven, out on the sand.

We watched the peculiar scene with the curiosity of a street-cat, and a Daygo police car arrived. I sprayed another layer of sunscreen on my flesh-coat—my mom would be proud—behind shades that shielded the perplexion in my eyes. The cop went inside E.S.'s beach-shack castle, and we leaned against the porch's brick-wall barrier to better assess the situation—riding high hopes that E.S. was alright.

Suddenly, with our stomachs in our throats, the medical workers came through the front door with a metal stretcher. On top was a full sack, like a bag of un-opened potato chips.

Our stomachs smashed to our bellies like a poorly timed duck-dive gets drilled deep, and Shanders dropped his ¾ full can-of-beer, making a loud, dense thud as the liquid dribbled out on the cement porch—the air in our lungs did the same into the beachside atmosphere.

"Excuse me, sir?" Sheezer—my other roommate—asked in bare feet, soles tough as shoes.

"What's up, man?" the medical worker said.

"Uhh, what's going on? Where's Steve?" Sheezer asked.

"He's gone...the rust got him. The beach will do that, ya know," the medical worker said, and they loaded the stretcher, locked it in place, and drove off because that's what ambulances do.

We were shocked, E.S. was gone, and that's what happens on the beach, when you live there long enough. Another casualty of the sandy-toed-life, so we sipped beers and felt stiff in the sun.

Caliguluck
laine perry

These are the wild times, nights of drinking, sunning ourselves, afternoons of decadent meals, and evenings of dirty sex we carefully avoided during our marriages. C. is my best friend. We share a willingness to triumph over the immense pain we've reaped and sown. We belong to each other, and to this town—this seaside amalgam of transient vessels, motion, sea, broken spirits, and fierce devotion waiting to attach. The light in our eyes is a trick that still works. We make our mistakes. We are knocked to our knees. We fall on slick, wet stones. Refusing to fall in two feet of water, we rise and continue toward the breaking waves. The dull ache: a welcome flagellation of bone.

These are dark times. These are the nights when we come to know brutality intimately. We engage in these nights to protest failed marriages. We are carving out a new beauty for ourselves. We are old. This town idealizes destroyed beauty. We will not leave this town for this reason. Each man here has known a woman like us at one time. They see beyond the truth of our age. They wear sadness like a hat. They know it is there defining them in some way and when they need to, they remove it. Our sadness is worn like skin. It is on us for good. On better days it shifts layers and heads deep.

My neighbor, the airbrush artist, tells me I am the new Henry Miller. This town is the tropic of everything unholy. At a point, the close streets converge. The Strand, which is German for beach (and includes blood, muck, and stringy saliva) runs along the ocean. Some afternoons we walk the Strand counting the number of men who say, "Hello," to us. I pat my beer belly and yell, "This wasn't easy. This took years. I don't even like beer." C. laughs. The men don't care about the belly. They like our breasts. They see our faces, and it makes them sad, and guilty, even wistful. Their own tattoos remind the men to take their shot and let us pass. I say I don't look at men, but I do hear their voices full of longing, broken faith, and hot, hot, heat.

The has-been, never-been, never-going-to-be old men, the male versions of us. They recline with a permanent squint on the corner with a tall can. They are beaten down. They don't destroy anything anymore. They drink it down. They swallow it deep. It's every lost woman, estranged child, dead friend, every house that went back to the bank, every car repossessed. It's the awards of merit and trophies stacked somewhere in a friend or brother's basement, all of this in the eyes. It's a spark in a squint, the fire still there alongside the repercussions of infamous resolutions, waves, and surfboards muddied with wax.

My house-sitting job is almost over. The people I work for are also clients at my art gallery. They will be back from Australia within the next day or so. I've drunk all their booze and eaten their food, including jars of expensive condiments they believed were safe. I've loved their house well for them.

I am homeless again in a couple of days. I'll be living in the gallery. If I didn't own the place I would not go back to work—ever. It's unbearable in the gallery with Jessee gone missing. He won't come back. I told him too many times he didn't do anything for business. He smoked outside the shop, littered his butts on the sidewalk, and drank his 40 oz in the window. He looks destroyed when he's with me and destroyed when he's not. He's now sleeping on couches and in skate parks, and other places. My breath is uneven in his absence. It's hung up by burrs.

Jessee's taken my New York Dolls CD with him, so I head out to replace it. In my haste, I waste thirty bucks on a live box set full of ambiance and little else. I think of artists who might possess the good stuff and hit up Tim. He burns *Live in Paris '97* for me along with my old favorite, Love (Arthur Lee) and some early Stooges. Listening to this makes me crazy. I ride Jessee's old Schwinn over to his job. On my way I see a chubby young guy on a weird bike. Love handles and ape hangers, I tell him, "My bike is cooler than yours." He laughs. I tell him I want to start a punk band. He says he's played in a punk band for ten years, took a hiatus and is ready to hit it again. He promises to come by the gallery and does. I hand him the song I've written for Jessee, who works behind love handles and ape hangers' apartment. He lays down some guitar and we have something. People are coming into the shop. They like what's going down. The next day I see Jessee hanging out a town over. I can't eat. The guitar player comes over and we try to play. A bass player shows up. I can't sing. I can only think of Jessee, the heat of him, his body close to mine. I drink so much I black out. I wake to find Chubby raping me. I throw up and he drags me to the bathroom.

In the morning C. and I find dead birds and blond hair everywhere. C. says, "Why exaggerate when the truth is so much more alarming?" The dead pigeon is on the front bumper of my neighbor's '56 Chevy truck. Two clumps of blonde hair are lying on the sidewalk just outside the gallery door. C. photographs both items to make a record of this time in our lives. "This is going to be a hell of a summer," she says. I need a turntable, and C. thinks she needs a dildo. To prepare for our mission we buy two bottles of red wine and more Mickey's beer because C. likes the puzzles on the flip side of the caps. The dildo is eighteen dollars. The clerk throws in the batteries. C. names it Ceasar (Ceasar the Pleaser). We head to the thrift store where C. pays fifteen dollars for my turntable because I am still penniless. She promises to volunteer at the thrift store where we found it. She likes the stories the manager tells her. The manager is 'coked up' and wears thick black mascara. I like the frenetic push she gives. It gets us out the door and to the grocery store. I want to buy beer in the unlikely event that he stops by to reconcile. C. goes home for her date with Caesar. Sadly, she manages to make off with the good bottle of red. What she leaves me with is affectionately known as, "two-buck chuck."

In the car the next morning, The Stones are screaming about the suburban bitch with faraway eyes. C. has those eyes. She finally takes me to her house in Corny-copia. It's one of those communities so lifeless if it wasn't for the cars in the driveways, you could be sure it was a ghost town. The whole thing looks like an abandoned project. Layers of dust cover up the barely intentional tan paint. I blink fast and the whole scene washes to a field of dirt. We're out of there in a hurry after feeding the perplexed cat and throwing seed toward the fledglings.

Just as we are abandoning the building she lives in, I spy a lime-green vintage dress hanging in her garage. My mom was a model in the sixties, and I can imagine her in that dress, raven hair piled high, black liner framing her stark blue eyes. I can hear my mother singing, "One less bell to answer—one less egg to fry..." C. looks at me looking at the dress and gives it to me. My neighbor Justin has an auto repair shop behind my art gallery. He is turning thirty tonight. I think I'll wear the lime to his party. I would marry Justin. I can't because he has C.P. and a lazy eye, and it makes me too sad to see that every minute of my life. All that laid out, he's still the best man in town.

Last night I dreamed I was riding in a car with some young kids. In the dream I saw a very large rattlesnake on the side of the road and pointed this out to the little ones.

They watched the snake. The driver sped up and so did the snake. The snake increased in size as we increased speed. His scaled skin was black and dark green. His eyes kept our look. He became ten feet tall, at a point stood upright as a human, and his two unnoticed hands began to spin a clear thread. He was spooling thread, and he was ten feet tall. That was how we left him. I'm not sure what his plans were at that point. I'm not sure what our destination had been. We drove on neither terrified nor prescient.

This afternoon is electric. I'm watching it. I have my eye on this afternoon—and for good reason. I'm drinking rum. I've drunk three-fourths of the contents of the glass already. It's 11:14 A.M. Ice cubes tinkling, I think of Esther, my grandmother. My soulmate. I can smell her skin, the warmth and dirt—the way she gave in. Her smell is in the drink. It's Sunday. The gig's up and I am back at the gallery. The tight jaws that pass by are headed toward a case of something I like to call "Epiphanitis." It's a made-up disease where every epiphany is also a macabre discovery.

A haggard artist with a relaxed jaw stops in to tell me he's been moving all day after giving up the fight with his girlfriend of fifteen years. He'd just rather give up their place on Fire Mountain and move to a little shack with a view of the ocean. He used to be a surfer. He used to be in the ocean every day. Then he fell in love and moved inland to raise a family. He tells me at the exact moment when he realized the significance of his loss, he ran as fast as he could to the ocean he had abandoned. As he stood before it, praying for his life's resolution, he noticed a group of younger people. They were humming, and crying, and throwing some things into the sea. The first thing he noticed was a wreath. When he blinked his remorse away, he saw the roses that had been thrown in after the wreath. They were a good twenty feet away but edging gingerly toward it. The roses kept steady on their target, achieving a union within three to five minutes. This impressed him like nothing else. As he marveled over such a simple miracle, he adjusted his focus to include the horizon. Two dolphins dove in an arc, framing the goodbye wreath with its rose arms and leafy absolution. He shuffled backward and finally turned away from the group. He had prayed for grace and found it. People had not done him much good until that moment.

I'm standing on the rotting porch of the house I'm sitting. It is late afternoon. After succumbing to a bout of hunger I open a tin of detested tuna, and sprinkle red-wine vinegar on it. I douse it with French mustard, and pepper it well. It's still tuna. I feel queasy rather than grateful after eating it. The four-year-old neighbor comes over. Her sniffer pointed high in the air, she announces, "The sky smells like rain!" Hmmm. "I'm making peach pie!" she says with a silly, proud smile. I want some. "It's made of dirt and sticks!" she says. "All right," I tell her. That said, she unpacks her little spoons and small cups. We eat our pie beneath a clear blue sky. She gives another sniff and packs up in haste. I duck inside to listen to the thunder of heavy rain on a metal roof.

Today in the shop the strumming sounds like picking. It's a tin guitar. Better blues than these? I have not known them. My neighbor O'Reilly Jones is crooning. It's not yet noon. The sky is silver and grey. He misses his brother who is a cold first tenor, crystal clear. He doesn't tell me how his brother was killed. He sits on my blue tufted pleather couch. He sits very still. I bring out a little amp I have stashed in back. His blue love songs are strokes across my chest, arousing me and tempting me to rise like a phoenix from the ashes of my last incarnation as art dealing skate-widow, beer swilling, over-the-hill vixen. He croons, "Eight men and twelve women found me guilty of loving you." In the nineties O'Reilly Jones was caught making love in a car in Houston, Texas. When they went to court, the judge asked his woman, "Tell me, do you really love that man?" His story breaks the dark cloud. The truth is that O'Reilly Jones has come to tell me he wants me. He's noticed that my old man has hit the road. He's wanting in. There's a prostitute strolling south toward the old man's business. I can hear the double click of heel on pavement. It is not so different from the heavy rain on the tin roof. O'Reilly Jones is taking Amtrak to L.A. He's been cast as James Brown in the upcoming Spike Lee film. I pop in Parliament and let the funk satisfy. I've had sex in a speeding car, but never anything stationary.

Tonight, I open a show at my art gallery. Three hundred people come to see the art. With the help of a talented chef, and a crucial D.J., I sell fifty-three paintings. This is a record. This is something that does not happen in Oceanside, California. My artist has come all the way from Washington D.C. He has one arm, and a tiny girlfriend. He is enamored of the beach town that has embraced him. He wants to move here. This is how it happens. I put on a Nina Simone album and beg him to reconsider.

Darkling

evan morgan williams

The principal saw us coming, and he set his coat and satchel on his desk. He pulled chairs for us at the table he kept for conferences. It was late on a Friday, and the light through the blinds was long. The principal sat down. He looked happy and sad at the same time.

"Miss Lim and Mrs. Dey!"

He turned to me. He rested his hand on the table. "Young lady, let's see your plans." He looked at me long enough to remind me of someone. "Going out on a Friday night? Lovely."

I had brushed my hair. In my classroom. Alone. Now I touched my hair where it curled under at my neck. My fingers smelled like sanitizer. I slid next week's lesson plans across the table. The principal reminded me of someone, a memory I had lost.

"Where's yours?" he said to Mrs. Dey.

"Right here, John." She slid her plan. "You already know what it says. And don't I get a 'lovely' too?"

The principal flipped through her plan, pages turning quickly. Sure, the plan was good enough. Mrs. Dey knew how do to this. Chapter Five of the textbook, *The Lottery*, the worksheets, the reader response, the writing sample. The principal seemed barely to read it.

Mrs. Dey said, "Don't look so excited, John."

"I'm not worried about you. I've seen your test scores."

Mrs. Dey rummaged through her purse for a compact. She began fixing herself up. She pulled out lipstick and perfume and set them on the table.

"No," said the principal, and he put his hand over her makeup. "Not here, not now. And for goodness sake, wherever you ladies go, hide your lanyards."

"You know where we're going, John," said Mrs. Dey. "You could come along. You know you used to."

The principal tilted toward me. He gazed at me. Then I knew. He reminded me of my favorite teacher when I was in school. The crisp blue business shirt, rumpled at the end of the day, no tie, no blazer. It was okay to be reminded of my favorite teacher. But he wasn't my favorite teacher. He placed his hand gently on my arm and said to Mrs. Dey, "This one here, I did not hire her so you could corrupt her with worksheets and cocktails." His gaze returned. "Now, my dear, what's yours again?" He rummaged for my lesson plans. They were on the bottom now.

"Literature conferences," I said. I watched my lesson plans rustling in his hands. He read slowly. He was taking too long. He said, "Are you going to put on makeup too? Yes? No? Not my business?" He looked up. "Now tell me about this plan so I don't have to read it."

"Okay. My students and I, we have these dialogues..."

"That doesn't sound like a lesson plan."

I knotted my fingers in my lap. "But it's carefully planned. There are literacy goals for every student. I'm thorough and detailed. It's not a dialogue actually, more like a conference."

He said, "Like we're having a conference right now."

I wanted to grab onto this, even though it wasn't correct. But he said, "I'm going to need more next time. I'd like to see these literacy goals."

Mrs. Dey muttered, "Easy does it, John." She reached for her lipstick.

He looked at us both. "Any kids getting lost lately?"

"I don't lose kids, John."

"Sure, you don't. I had Luis Martinez in here today, and he was sobbing."

"Luis will abide."

Myself, I lost kids every day. I'd like to believe I found them again. Maybe through the books we read together. But how to say that? What was my data? Did Luis have a good book? Who could I talk to about my students? Mrs. Dey? This man?

He said, "Miss Lim, the literature conferences are a fine idea. If you can pull them off. But you're young. I'd like to come and see."

Mrs. Dey whispered not to worry. She stood. I stood. I felt better. It was going to be a relief to go out on a Friday night. Teachers in tired cardigans. Sure. Okay.

The principal smiled. He was happy now, without the sad. He said, "I'm serious, Dey, don't do anything scandalous with this one. I hired her myself. I have a special interest here."

I laughed, because laughing was one of the choices, and it seemed like the best one.

The parking lot was dark and almost empty. The custodian's car. The principal's car. My car. Mrs. Dey's.

She said, "First stop, The Hot Tot."

"The what?"

"The nail salon in the strip mall. Then we'll hit the bar. You want good nails when you hit the bar. The light, the mirrors, the shiny bottles, you want to dazzle. You want good nails. I'm telling you this since you do not know. You have your ID?"

"Because Asian girls get carded all the time?"

Mrs. Dey patted my arm. She turned for her car.

I said, "So did you and the principal have a thing, you know, a moment?"

She waved off my question. "The past is the past, honey."

We drove our separate cars to the Hot Tot. You didn't carpool. You didn't leave your car in the empty school lot in the evening. In this job, it turns out, you didn't do anything alone except to drive your car and dwell in your thoughts at how much you'd messed up another day. That was always alone. No one to talk to. No one to listen. We made it to The Hot Tot, and I did my makeup in the visor mirror alone.

The inside of the salon was dimly lit except for the stations with their small bright lamps. There were scraps of light from the parking lot's tall lamps, and the beaming headlights of passing cars, spilling in like noise, and the potted plants caught the light upon their leaves. Beyond the plants, there were three manicure stations brightly lit beneath work lamps, cones of light against black Formica, and your eye went to them.

I said, "Don't we need an appointment?"

Mrs. Dey said, "I already phoned in."

An older woman called from her station. "Mrs. Dey! You bring your teacher friend! Come! We make you pretty for your students." We stepped closer. There was a second older woman at the station on the right, and a younger woman at the station on the left. They said nothing. They did not even turn. They were not in the light.

The woman who called to us was seated in the cone of light at her station. She was small, with a smooth smiling face. She wasn't so old. Her hair was thinning, and maybe that's what made her look old. She wore a long silk blouse and leggings. She had a surgical mask dangling from one ear. She said, "Mrs. Dey, your friend is so pretty. We make you both pretty."

Mrs. Dey leaned close to me. Her perfume was fresh. She took my arm and leaned even closer. We were not in the light. "This is such a stereotype, Jenny. You know that funny video online, the lady comedian in the nail salon? Oh gosh, I'm sorry if that offends you."

I said, "I'm not Vietnamese, if that's what you mean."

"Okay."

"Yes. Okay."

Mrs. Dey sat at the woman's station. She laid her hands on the black table in the bright light. "School colors, Mrs. Nguyen! Blue and gold."

I sat next to her. The stations were very close. The nail artist at my station was much younger. She looked my age. She was sorting tools in a plastic drawer. She turned and gave me a nod.

"Hello," I said.

"Hey."

At the third station, an old woman watched from the edge of her lamp light and said nothing.

Mrs. Dey's woman said, "We make you pretty, like sisters."

"Oh Christ!" cried Mrs. Dey.

My girl leaned toward me over her table. She looked at me, then she looked away, in and out of the light. She wore a black t-shirt, black jeans, and a black lace choker. She took my hands, flipped them over, and stroked my wrist, down to my palm, then stroked each of my fingers separately. Her nails were long and glossy black in the lamp's brilliant shine. She wore her long hair forward around her face, like she was hiding in it, shiny and black.

Mrs. Dey was watching. She didn't miss. Her face brightened. She said, "Hello Pashae, my little Darkling."

The girl, Pashae, slumped. "Hey, Mrs. Pumpkin Spice." She looked back to my hands and rubbed my fingertips one by one. It felt amazing.

"I had Pashae in my class. I had her sister too. See, I called Pashae my darkling and she called me—"

The woman doing Mrs. Dey's nails cut in. "And her mother too. You don't forget me! Teacher! I always say you are Mrs. Day, so I am Mrs. Night." She laughed.

"Always good to see you, Mrs. Nguyen. Call us madcap teachers, but it's girls' night out, and—"

"Girls' night out? You know I have my special thing for you." Mrs. Nguyen reached under her table and produced a whiskey bottle and tiny plastic cups. She poured shots of Jim Beam. "A special night for teachers!"

"I love this place!" Mrs. Dey handed me one of the plastic cups.

The woman without a customer took one of the cups. Everyone took a cup.

Mrs. Dey knocked back her cup of whiskey and filled another. "How old are you now, Darkling?

Pashae said, "Twenty-three."

"Jenny, do you hear that? She's just like you. I had her sister Alice, and I had Pashae. Alice was a shining star!"

"Was I a star too, Mrs. Pumpkin Spice?"

"Of course you were!"

Pashae didn't say anything.

The older women didn't say anything.

"Oh, that's right. I'm so sorry."

Pashae put on her mask. She said, "That's okay. Anyway, she was my half-sister. I'm surprised you remember her. Most people have forgotten." She applied a strong-smelling gel to remove my old polish, pink and flat, chipped and worn.

Mrs. Dey drank her second pour. She fluttered her fingers. "Make them nice and long, Mrs. Nguyen. For grading papers! For cocktails!"

Maybe it had been a mistake to mention the sister. Pashae and her mom settled into their work and didn't talk. The third woman stared toward the windows, the lights of the passing cars, white and red, headlights and brakes. In the silence, you noticed the music playing in the shop.

Asian pop music. Vietnamese? I couldn't tell. Pashae said nothing. She scraped off the old polish, gooey with gel, and dug at my cuticles, my tired teacher cuticles. She rubbed my hands gently. I was falling into a trance. It was so quiet, and there was the music, and I felt I had to be quiet. I whispered, "That thing about school colors? Please, no. Pink will do."

Pashae scuffed the surface of my nails with a tiny whirring instrument.

She said, "You're not Vietnamese."

"I'm Cambodian."

"The land of lost souls." She dug with a flat edged tool.

"Literally no one says that."

"But you won't forget it now."

Pashae's body relaxed, and her hands working on mine relaxed, and my hands relaxed as well, and we were falling under the same spell. Not falling, but floating. It was so quiet that I felt there was just the two of us in the world, leaning into the cone of bright light from the lamp at her station, and the light was warm on my face.

She said, "So do you teach math? Music? Science? What?"

"I teach reading. I teach books."

"I liked books."

"Which ones."

"*The Hunger Games* series. It's stupid, I know."

"That's not stupid. There is a lot to learn from them."

"How do you make someone want to learn?"

"Like this, talking, like we're doing right now."

She lifted her tool and looked at me. Her eyes peered over her mask.

She said, "I used to like books. Not anymore."

I said, "I bet you loved *The Hunger Games*. Then you found out other kids loved it too. And it kind of ruined your special love. I'm sorry, I don't know you. That was just a guess. Anyway, there is some good writing there. We can talk about her authorial choices. Like, why do you think she put it in the present tense?"

It was a teacher question. Pashae and I had stumbled into a literature conference. I didn't know any other way to talk to someone.

Pashae said, "I don't remember it being in the present tense. That was a long time ago. And what's it to you? I stopped reading. I don't read."

It all started with my favorite teacher. He had given us books and asked us all about them. We had to have evidence, post-in notes sticking out from the pages of *The Great Gatsby*. But my notes, I remember, they didn't have answers, only questions. Like I had written, "Why am I supposed to care about these people?" So, my favorite teacher and I found a way forward. I didn't remember what it was. I didn't remember the book. The point is I remembered the person who helped me try.

Mrs. Dey said, "You girls are certainly getting along. Is she giving you a hard time?"

I came back from where we'd been and said, "Which one of us do you mean?"

She laughed and again she cried out, "Christ!" I think she would have poured herself more whiskey, but Pashae's mom had control of her hands and was working calmly, an artist's concentration. The third woman reached for the bottle and poured more shots for everyone. Mrs. Dey eyed her fresh shot. I had not touched mine.

Pashae said, "Okay. I also liked *The Lovely Bones*. I loved it. Maybe I'd read that again."

Mrs. Dey was quiet. She wasn't laughing anymore. She watched Pashae's mom working over her hands. Then she watched Pashae. Her voice went soft. "Alice loved *The Lovely Bones*. She was a special one. Of course, you both were special. But she was my shining star."

"I don't really know how she was in school. She was quite a bit older, you see." Pashae applied a base coat with a tiny brush. Her hands were smooth and pale and soft. Her nails were shiny black. I was utterly relaxed, melting, slumped, the quiet, the music, the light, the smell of whiskey around me, the end of a long week at school. Luis Martinez, sobbing in the hall. What had I done wrong?

"Alice probably told you about *The Lovely Bones*. Gosh, seeing you reminds me of her."

Pashae said, "We were not the same. Do you really think we look the same? We were half-sisters. I'm surprised you think we look the same at all."

"I'm talking about the cuteness, the Gothy stuff. It's very quaint. Did you get that from her as well? Oh, I wish I could hug her right now. Your sweet sister. I sat her in the back of the class so as not to play favorites."

"I was in the back of the class. Was I a favorite too?"

"I'll never tell. I don't play favorites."

"My sister was everyone's favorite."

"No! I forged a special relationship with her. She even did my nails, you know. Gosh, she was exceptional. Beautiful work. Then she got out of this life. Went to college and got out. I wrote her a letter of recommendation. I even mentioned the sister in *The Lovely Bones*, the one who was a go-getter. A teacher notices those things."

Pashae had stopped her work on my hands. We had lost the place we had been, floating in the light. "So, she did your nails. Interesting. But you mustn't put too much stock in her work. I did your nails once too. One Saturday afternoon when my sister couldn't come in. She was already having trouble. Perhaps you can remember. Maybe you're mixing us up. The masks and all. You did say we looked alike."

"I would remember if you did my nails, Darkling."

"I offered black and dark red."

"Blue and gold!" she cried. "Never mind. I know you're busy now. You work so hard, Pashae!"

The third woman spoke up. "I do your nails too."

The light of a police car sped by.

Mrs. Dey waved both her hands. Pashae's mom had to pull back. Pashae pulled back too. Mrs. Dey went on. "We planned out dreams. High school, the zine club, the theater club, college! She made me love my job. We read so many books. We literally memorized them. What did she learn? Didn't matter! You can find it all on the internet now. But Alice found new books for me. The dog-eared pages. The notes. She pressed so hard. That should have been a sign. Sometimes her notes said only, 'This! This!' And I read her books. I kept her safe. I remember a hug in her graduation dress. Dear sweet girl. Elation, that's what I remember. I miss her. Because that was so long ago. One wants to live it all again. The perfection of the moment when time stopped and you changed the world. Not the world, but one girl's world."

Everybody felt uncomfortable. I felt knocked loose. I had been so calm.

The third woman poured more whiskey and said something in Vietnamese.

Pashae's mom replied. She drank down her cup of whiskey.

Mrs. Dey said nothing. She downed her cup.

Pop music, soft and blurry. It led me back in...

Pashae leaned very close, and the heat I felt was hers. She resumed her work on my nails. "You don't talk about the past. You don't regret the past, and you don't worry about the future. I do my job. I make some money. I eat, I sleep, I do this. Right here. Right now."

She held my fingertips under a special lamp, then began to apply the glossy pink.

"During math and science and social studies, and lunch and recess and the bus ride home, pretty much the entire day, I sat alone and snuck out *The Lovely Bones*. I kept my head down and hid inside my hair. I could drag my fingernail along the dark, beautiful story."

"You just said not to talk about the past."

She held my nails, glimmering glossy pink, beneath the special lamp to dry. She reached in her drawer and pulled out a tiny brush, delicate as floss, brilliant silver, white and fine.

The stations were very close together, those three cones of light. I could feel Mrs. Dey watching. I could smell her whiskey breath. Pashae spoke just above a whisper. "I'm pretty sure it was one of my teachers who turned me in. Turned in my mom, I mean. Foster care was only a few weeks, but you block out the hard times, don't you. You make what happiness you can. Anyway, of course it was the right thing to do."

Our heads were touching in the warmth of the light. Floating? More like adrift.

I offered, "I had a teacher who cared about me very much. He gave me books..."

Pashae's voice was muffled through her mask. "I'm the one who hid the knives. I'm the one who flushed the pills. I took away the car keys. I'm the one who stayed awake. The real reason I began to read..." She pointed to the tray of adornments for the flashiest nails, tiny wings, stars, jewels. "I did her nails. I made her hands useless as a barbie doll's. Long and thick, heavy and curled. She couldn't make a fist or grip a razor blade. She couldn't turn the ignition of our car. She couldn't open the bottle of those pills that were supposed make her feel nothing at all."

The tiny brush flickered on my nails. The range of Pashae's motions were tight within the lamp's light. I fought to get back my calm. I had no wish to guide the conversation. I had no goals. Pashae had no goals. But it would have been nice to be able talk this way. I never got to be the one to talk. My mom and I had arguments. We were playing roles. My dad was completely out of the picture. But even if I got to be the talker, I had nothing to say. If you knew Cambodia, you knew what I meant. There was nothing. And with the students, it was only listening. But if I were doing the talking, what would I say? I was completely new to teaching. I felt new to life. I had nothing. Maybe that was the thing I needed to say.

Pashae brought me back. She said, "What did they expect would happen while I was gone?"

Mrs. Dey leaned to listen.

Pashae's work became smaller and smaller. Those tiny brush strokes. I felt her breathe in, breathe out. I breathed with her, floating in shallow water.

"So, my sister, she called me when I was in foster care. She said, 'Be a good girl, Pashae.' She said, 'Don't listen to Mom. Don't be that kind of good girl. There is a different kind of good girl, and you are that good girl, and I am not. Just be that kind of good girl.'"

"So pretty, blue and gold." Pashae's mom was wrapping up with Mrs. Dey.

Pashae was still painting. Tiny white lines, arcs and slashes. I realized they were characters in a language I could not read.

"I got my cosmetology certificate. And here I am. Because I know what the future contains. An end. You teachers speak in promises. You don't talk about the ending part. That's why I stopped reading books. They always end. The point is I stopped finishing them."

Mrs. Dey stood. Pashae still wasn't done. I turned to Mrs. Dey. "I'll catch up. I will."

"I can wait." Mrs. Dey watched quietly over us. There was a long silence. We all watched Pashae's tiny brush, thin as a human hair. Then Mrs. Dey spoke. Her voice was soft and close. "That was a long time ago."

Pashae paused with her fine brush. She looked up and out of the light. She found Mrs. Dey in the dark. She shook back her long hair. "Not so long, really. And here I am, sucking fumes in a nail salon."

Mrs. Dey's voice was both firmness and care. "Pashae, I'm not dense. I get why you're still here. You think I don't get it, but you don't know. So, guess what? I will tell you. We have a student, Luis. He wears a long loose hoodie you could camp inside. And he always has to borrow a pencil to complete a thought. He presses so light. He gives the pencil back. But the things he writes. I hope he can be happy, but it's hard to be happy, don't you know. And I read his journal, and I find out he lost his dad to drunk driving. He didn't really know his dad, but this almost made it worse. Now he checks in with me every day. And I listen to every word. Of course you didn't know about this. Because you never asked. Here, look at me. Can you tell? No. Why not? Because I get on with life. Luis gets on with life. We try to, anyway. We carry our pain. You think I don't know about pain, honey, but you have no idea. And I have a hundred more kids like Luis. It's okay to be hopeful. Anyway, it's really not your business."

"So maybe I'm not your business, either."

"A student's business is always a teacher's business. Remember what Walt Whitman said? We read his poem, and I know you remember."

"He contained multitudes?"

"Good girl. A teacher contains multitudes."

"Okay, Mrs. Dey, but I also remember reading Hemingway. This salon is my *Clean Well-Lighted Place*. The light upon the leaves..."

"You're a good girl, and your sister was a very good girl." Mrs. Dey turned, twittering her glistening fingers, blue and gold. She paid Mrs. Nguyen and left the salon. I overheard her stepping out the door, saying to no one. "My shining star!"

Pashae was wrapping up with me. She glued tiny sparkling jewels around the silky character designs. I didn't want them, but I didn't want this to end, so I let her go on. I didn't want to go drinking at the flashy bar. I wanted this. Pashae said, "With this set, you'll have to be careful. Don't touch anything for a while. Let it dry. Do not pull on or off your sweater. You have to let it dry into something solid. And practical. I mean, this is not practical at all. For a teacher, it is lavish. But it is only a small thing. And you have to be both girly and tough. Look, that old lady, she's not so bad. How do you think she's made it this long? And the girls in your special reading conferences, when you talk about books, they will take your hands. I'm serious. They'll take your hands and say your name, all fakey Asian like, "Miss Jenny! You so pretty!"

Pashae's mom and the older woman were pouring shots and sipping slowly, in and out of the light, talking softly, calmly, smoothly.

"This set will last for weeks. It will grow out from the cuticle, of course. Come back then, and we'll talk some more. Maybe it will be your turn."

"But I have nothing. Maybe I have one thing. But it was in the past."

"It's not about the past. It's not about the future, either. That's the trick, you see."

I said, "So what does it say on my nails?"

"This one says, 'I won't kill myself today.' This one says, 'I don't need to complete anything.' This one says, 'Nobody is beautiful.' Then I run out of things to say."

"You don't really know that. Vietnamese doesn't even use characters."

"Okay, I made them up."

"What do I owe you? This looks expensive."

"We put it on Mrs. Dey's card."

I admired my beautiful new nails. I imagined my sparkling fingertips guiding the eye along the words upon a page. And I said something new. I found a Mrs. Dey thing to say. And by saying a Mrs. Dey thing, my spell was broken. "My students will be so pleased. I'll tell them I met Pashae."

Pashae laughed. She put away her tools. She took off her mask. She wiped her beautiful mouth on a tissue.

I said, "It has been a lovely evening. These first few weeks have been hard for me. Nobody to talk to. I can finally say that I'm happy again. I don't know, something like happy."

"Happy and sad? You can be both at the same time, you know."

We didn't hug. We didn't shake hands. We didn't bow. Nothing. There was nothing to complete between us. It was all very practical. Pashae reached for the switch and turned off her lamp. I left for the darkness that led to the sparkling shiny bar.

Baby Girl
lenore weiss

My new family signed the adoption papers. Their apartment building was filled with brass banisters and red velvet wallpaper that hadn't been updated since the end of World War I, the kind of building where Rosemary's Baby might've taken its first breath. Mom greeted the doorman and pressed the elevator button to the 20th floor.

Ballentine, my brother, welcomed me home. Wearing Bermuda shorts, his legs were the color of uncooked spaghetti, mine like whole wheat pasta. We sat on his bed and binged episodes of Star Trek. He told me his family had lost a baby to something called sudden death while her mobile had played *Ba Ba Black Sheep* above her head.

"She was around for two weeks. I heard her cry." Ballentine removed a shoebox from beneath his bed and let me look at his baseball cards.

In those first years, all went well. But around middle school, I started to hear voices, soft rustlings at first, calling my name. *Emily. Wake up, you sluggard!* The voice persisted. Get up! You'd think that I'd look under my bed for monsters or pull a pillow over my head. I did neither. Foster care had steeled me for such occasions. The sound was coming from the ceiling.

Hey, little girl. I'm talking to you. What are you doing in my bed?

I yanked the covers up to my chin, hoping it was only Ballentine trying to scare me three weeks before Halloween hit all the stores.

"Excuse me. What d'you mean by your bed?"
Don't you know who I am?

I screamed. Mom dashed into my room and told me to go to sleep. That didn't stop my nightmares. They only became worse.

During a Star Trek episode, I cried to Ballantine that my adopted parents might turn me back into the agency as a defective part.

"Won't happen, Em. They're stuck with you."

By now, I was eleven and Ballantine was fourteen. But miraculously, over the next few months things got better. Ballantine gave me an extra set of ear buds to block out the voice. But I could still hear her rolling around in the ceiling.

One evening, I spoke directly to it. "Who are you?"

The wind howled and shook the windows on the 20th floor of our apartment building.

My breath quickened. "What do you want?"

It's me, doofus, Baby Girl.

"Who taught you to talk?"

You think I'm stupid? I've been listening all these years through the ceiling.

We stayed up together. Baby Girl shared her early days. She wondered if I knew what had happened to her mobile with the cute fluffy sheep. I didn't have a clue.

"Sorry, Baby Girl. Before my time."

I hoped Baby Girl had gotten the answers she needed to find peace. As for me, Mom enrolled me in an inner-city day camp where we had contests about who could pick up the most litter in yellow garbage bags. I entertained the kids during snack with Star Trek episodes. I'd memorized them all. Time well spent with Ballantine.

At the end of summer, a boy at camp invited me to a birthday party in his backyard.

The food was laid out on a wooden slat—propped up on cinder blocks at either end—and covered with a paper tablecloth that read "Happy Birthday." There were two kinds of salad—macaroni and green olive—and coolers of soda. Presents in bows and colorful paper were stacked behind the tree while friends and family gathered in hues of mocha to mahogany—just like me.

Chester shouted, "Drumroll! Emily! You're on."

All week I'd been practicing. I did all my Star Trek voices including Lieutenant Uhura: "If it isn't done right, I could blow the entire communications system…"

Everyone laughed. "You sound just like Uhura."

For weeks afterward, I heard no more Baby Girl. I became friendly with the kids from camp. But one evening. I heard her.

You're not me. I should be you.

She tried to smother me with my own pillows. I wrestled with her.

"You're stone dead, Baby Girl. But you're right. I'm nothing like you. I'm not ready to throw in my baby blanket. You're dead and there's no double do-overs."

Something exploded, and through the ceiling, I heard a tinkly version of *Ba, Ba Black Sheep* before everything became quiet.

POETRY

Ode to a Book in the Ten Dollar All You Can Bag Book Sale

merridawn duckler

Massive amounts of underlining and several mismatched
indent brackets, paragraphs bled red with squiggles
free-hand five-point stars, question marks, eraser dust
double underscores, often the word *loneliness* circled
in wondrous dusky graphite. I knew a man read
with his finger holding the line of thought and I'll hold
the page so close my nose detects the sea of ink ahead.
Hanna Indecipherable Last Name, you summon
in cursive with flowers on the dotted *I*
that book of poems I bought deep in teenage waste-
land and filled with red ghosts, writing over the old forms,
to close the circle of childhood with the pleading, editing hand.

Scrabble

shobha tharoor srinivasan

She has no filter,
but she has no guile as well.
Her words tumble out of her
like shape blocks from an open can.
Sometimes they are tender,
telling stories of your sweetness as a child.
Yet often, she speaks the harsh truth:
that your girth has widened,
and you are looking fat.
"Go out and run" she says,
forgetting that when you leave her side
she calls out in plaintive howls—repeatedly.
Every night, whiskey in hand she asks for Scrabble.
Today she counts out six tiles: REPEAT
And places them on a triple word score.
A smile lights up her face.
"I have only studied up to high school" she says.
"What will you, with your multiple degrees, do?
I place MOTHER on the board.
Love is the only rule in this game.

My Soul is in the Bottom Drawer

ian day

of the file cabinet in the guest room closet
next to where the kitty litter used to be
and underneath the Halloween costumes.
There's my passport and birth certificate
and social security card and files of poems
and bad ideas. I had nowhere to send them:
the poems of course so I let them fill this metal
box like the tin man's chest. I guess I forgot
papers only flutter when thrown into the wind.

Hierarchy

joanna scandiffio

the day Ferlinghetti died   Tiger Woods crashed his car
You know who would got top billing   the one
whose car rolled over and over   his body had to be lifted
from the wreck with iron jaws   then rushed
to a hospital where everyone waited and wondered
if he could still play the game
Ferlinghetti who launched a thousand poets
published Ginsberg's "Howl"   the book that was declared
not fit for print   died quietly in his sleep
with no one asking
how he turned our minds upside down

Komorebi

alexandra bergmann

I didn't know what to call you
in my own tongue,
so I borrowed from another.

I didn't know how to call you
without a phone or number,
so I went to the forest at morning.

I'm told not to leave a trace,
a grace you won't grant me.

I'm told, if you traded leaves
for clouds, you'd be god rays.

Pacific Ocean
joshua kepfer

I   wonder   why   the   ocean   holds   so   much
wonder   for   us.   Pacific   dares   me   to   wonder
why   us?   Don't   animals   find   the   appeal   of
the   Pacific? Animals   swim   deep,   fly   to   horizons.
Ocean   dares,   find   deep   waters   in   God.   God
holds   me,   the   fly,   in   his   reach.   And
so,   to   appeal   to   God,   reach   for   the
much   wonder   of   horizons; God   and   the   ocean.

NONFICTION

Leonard Cohen Hated Me (Maybe Not)

lance mazmanian

Los Angeles, 1992: I used to go to Leonard Cohen's place once a week or so, to help navigate and refine his computer, a Macintosh SE/30. Cohen adopted the Apple Mac experience early on and used it extensively for his original artworks. He was pretty killer with a WACOM tablet, too.

Yes, Leonard Cohen and I shared many a late night together. Way more than mere tech. We'd often spend hours lost in obscure art, food, philosophy, tea, and so on.

We even planned a future writing collaboration. A chapbook, maybe. Cohen loved that I was a smalltime internationally published poet in my early twenties. He thought the work was "...very visual; quite excellent, indeed, especially for one so young." Ha! Seems silly to think of now.

Believe it or not, at the time in L.A., I had no idea who Leonard Cohen even was. To me, he was an unknown older cat who'd done a little poetry of his own, plus a few obscure vinyl records in the day. He seemed the average, middle-aged dude living solo in a cool pad stocked with books, paintings, hippie relics, and fancy eats. No understanding, on my side, to match his name with the legacy.

I feel right stupid about it now, of course. And as it went, our friendship was not to last.

You see, on a particular visit to his apartment/studio one crystalline L.A. eve, I caused Cohen to lose a huge stash of his personally created digital still life images. His "gems" as he called them: Nudes, portraits, landscapes.

Originals, of course. All of them painstakingly crafted using the latest Apple Macintosh tools of the era. No backups, either. All gone. Forever.

Oy.

These works were incredibly precious to Cohen, and God only knows where they might've shown by now: MoMA, Brett Wesley Gallery, Musée du Louvre...

Realistically, Cohen shared equal fault in it all—and though I shoulda been way more careful, what Cohen had going was totally unorthodox.

Leonard Cohen, while sharp with a WACOM tablet, and Photoshop and Painter too, really had no idea about the Apple proprietary interface. Thus, instead of hitting "Save" and storing his files as one would normally do, he was cutting and pasting his completed digital artwork right into the Mac's "Scrapbook" desk accessory.

The Scrapbook was a nifty 80s Apple holdover, intended for things used in a more or less repetitive manner: signatures, logos, notes, all available for quick placement to application files, via the desk accessory under the Apple menu (the little bitten fruit icon in the upper left).

But mid-1992, nobody really used Apple Scrapbook anymore.

Except for Leonard Cohen.

(Kidding about that...but not by far.)

Continuing:

Cohen had some serious Apple tech problems one day, so I came by at night, and low-level formatted his hard disk and custom reinstalled his System Software. Part of this process involved removing the Scrapbook's external storage, which Apple called "Scrapbook File." This item was kept inside the System Folder itself, and back then, the Scrapbook File would sometimes corrupt and cause the computer to hang—if the Scrapbook was even opened.

But nobody really used the Scrapbook anymore, right?

Except for Leonard Cohen.

As it went, I sat there in front of his SE/30, just a couple small steps from erasing the disk. Copied all his files to an external drive, ready to go.

But something felt off when I noticed the Scrapbook File was much larger than normal. So, I opened the Scrapbook itself. Inside were duplicates of Cohen's art, images I'd seen for weeks. I thought it was odd for him to have so many (all?) of these pics in the Scrapbook. Hm.

I checked his "Work" folder: Lots of TIFF files (images), many of them labeled with names like those in the Scrapbook. Okay, duplicates. "So, Leonard…you don't actually use the Scrapbook for anything, do you?"

He leaned into the screen. "No idea what that is," he said.

My response? "Alright, cool."

Yeah, I *shoulda* left the Scrapbook open, and I *shoulda* made completely sure he visually associated the Scrapbook with the Scrapbook File.

But nobody used the Scrapbook anymore…it was said.

I continued the overhaul, erased the disk, custom reinstalled the 1992 OS from scratch. The computer ran fantastically afterward: much quicker, completely error free, very clean.

Cohen was happy as hell, and extremely thankful. Problems that plagued him were gone, and he loved some of the organic rearranging I did for him (a paradigm that would later become my personal trademark in the Apple world).

Yes, Leonard Cohen, *the* Leonard Cohen, was excited and back to work. He couldn't wait to cut a check for my time…until he clicked the Scrapbook.

"Where's my work?!" he cried. I pointed to his Work folder, which I'd safely returned to his drive. "Right there. Back where it was," I said.

"No, no, no! My *work!*"

I was confused. "Leonard, the Work folder's right there!"

"No! Look!" He flipped through the Scrapbook's pages. In 1992 there were probably six default samples in the Scrapbook, things like a cartoon palm tree and a smiley face. The silly tone of these stock Apple pics was salting the Cohen wounds by the second.

"They're gone! They're all gone!!" he yelled. And finally, I got what he was talking about. *Uh, oh.*

"Leonard, you've been saving your work in the *Scrapbook?* Then what're all these files in the Work folder?"

"I don't know about those, and I don't care! My work's gone! It's all gone!"

So, there we sat, his files toast. He was utterly devastated. Mortified. Enraged. A few beats later, he suddenly stands and says, "You should leave. Yes, you have to leave."

In a fit of angry tears, Leonard Cohen, the Leonard Cohen, threw me out of his pad and into the night.

I neither saw, nor heard from him again.

Walking back to the car, I thought about offering a disk recovery, using the tools of the day. But the drive was erased by a low-level security wipe, so recovery was likely impossible, save for divine intervention or ekpyrotic fold.

I forgot about Cohen over the years. As I said, to me he was just an older dude who sang songs and made some art. It was not until 2006 I came to realize what Cohen's work had actually meant to the canvas of history:

Yes, I was at Sunset 5 movie theatre in L.A. (gone) waiting for some indie or another. Lights go down, a trailer for the documentary LEONARD COHEN: I'M YOUR MAN hits the screen. What the hell? *Leonard Cohen?* Why would anyone do a feature doc about *that* guy?!

In 2006, I had 14,000+ tracks in iTunes (now known as Apple Music): the great composers, movie music, jazz, obscure bands, popular rock and punk. A vast cross-section of near everything relevant since the year 1600.

Except for Leonard Cohen. Damn.

I Don't Know How to Pronounce Bolognese

bee lazar

My older and only sister is visiting, and she wanted to make Bolognese today. ~~My~~ Our mom went out and bought the ingredients and everything. Even at twenty-seven, my sister isn't much of a cook—in fact, one time she cooked lentils in her own flat back in Amsterdam, and they ended up on the walls and ceiling and painted the landlord-white surroundings a nice pea green. So I thought I'd do all the cooking myself; that way she wouldn't have to do any work. But she came into the kitchen and asked me, "do you want help?" This is how we ended up with her painfully uneven chops of onions far too big to be comfortable. I showed her my chopped half of the onion (which, arguably, could have been done better, but it was still diced small enough to cook quickly in medium heat) and she said, "they literally look the same," when they absolutely, most definitely did not look the same.

I just laughed and said, "okay, well, as long as you're fine with taking a bite of your Bolognese and getting a fucking big, huge bite of onion in it too," and she said, "yeah, that's fine, whatever," and, as I correctly guessed, she, in fact, did not fix her poorly chopped onions. But that's okay. Onions are still onions and are still good even if they're cut to be the size of your thumb. And when we cooked them with the garlic, she said "this is literally the best smell in the world," so it really didn't matter much in the end.

My sister is vegetarian, so my our mom bought a bag of fake ground beef, and we dumped it in after we'd let the carrots, celery, garlic, and onions cook for a bit. We stared at the brown lumps for a while until my sister said, "the recipe says to wait until the meat starts releasing juices," and

I said, "dude, I don't think that's gonna happen." So, we just waited. And waited. And dumped in so much Italian seasoning. And salt. "Too much salt is bad for you," she warned me. And I said, "you know what else is bad for you. Food that tastes like cardboard." So, after a brief moment of silence, she added more salt.

I don't see my sister often these days. Or ever, really. We have never been particularly close. When I was in high school, she was living in San Diego for college, and once she finished and came back, it was my turn to go off to university in Vancouver. That's, what, around seven or eight years of being far away from one another? And once I finished University, she moved away to live in Amsterdam. We have never been around for each other's adult lives, and so sometimes trying to talk to my sister feels more like talking to a stranger I've only ever seen pictures of.

With hands on the handle of the pot, she said, "I'm gonna add the noodles into the sauce now," and I responded with, "okay, just make sure you do it slowly," and turned away for one minute to check on ~~my~~ our dog. When I turned back around, she had dumped the entire pot of noodles into the pan of sauce and spilled a handful of them on the stove top. And it made me laugh, and I said, "sorry, I should've clarified that 'slowly' meant little by little batches of noodles. Not the speed at which you pour."

Sometimes I can't tell if I'm bad with instructions or if she just lacks common sense. I feel like it's a combination of both. Symbiosis has never really agreed with us, and yet, here we are, somehow grown from the same root.

When she was in high school and I was in middle school, I watched my sister rapidly grow thinner. I saw her shoulder bones jut high out of her body. I saw her rib cage strain against her skin, its outline clear enough I could count each rung. I saw her use small plates instead of big ones, the old "tricking yourself into believing you're eating a full meal by giving yourself a full plate while the plate is really small" trick, and then eventually, it became no plate at all. I saw her become small, so small, if you cut her open, there would be no more blood left to bleed.

To this day, whenever she picks up any packaged snack, she immediately checks the nutrition facts and consumes based off calculation. My sister, once a force so immovably big, became so infinitesimal she almost disappeared. With a sharpened want, she whittled herself to be close to nothing. And when you are a little girl, you want nothing more than to be like your older sister.

There we were, though, cooking together through the light of some divine exaltation, fighting through the thick, awkward silence in a rare effort to bridge the divide. The fake meat did not release any juices because it was not meat, that's kinda the whole point of it. But it was fine for the both of us because I was vegetarian for three years, and she continues to be to this day. Food for the both of us was in the saucepan, food we knew we were going to eat because we chopped the vegetables for it ourselves. When she said, "we should have something else to complement it," it felt like a miracle, this suggestion, this willingness. She is still small, smaller than I will ever be, but she is no longer see-through. To be at least tangible is enough for now.

My sister is twenty-seven and once ended up with lentils on her ceiling because she had the guts to stave off her hunger. Her onion chops are way too big, but she will still eat them regardless. When she goes to the fridge to find bread and cheese for some sides, I quietly add more salt to the Bolognese. She needs to increase her sodium intake anyway.

A Tale of Two Mothers

kristy webster

When your lover reads your poetry collection, you expect questions. Your writing is scathing—a rebellion of what you were taught, and everything you were groomed to be. You are most harsh towards your learned version of God, and your mother. You expect the poem where your mother threatens suicide with you and your sister in the car, to horrify him the most. You're surprised when he's gutted by the following lines:

Or how she threw the piano organ
you saved up for in the dumpster because
you would only embarrass yourself.

You're shocked at the way this detail disrupts his usually unflappable nature. You finally ask why, and he tells you, "To take a child's passion is devastating. It is the cruelest form of abuse in my opinion, and that is breaking a child's spirit. A child's spirit is sacred."

Months later, you also tell him when you were very young, you spent a year writing a book of poetry. You knew the poems were controversial. Still, you were excited to share them with your mother. You thought your submission and obedience, your excellent grades, and your Bible reading, would protect you. You handed your mother your manuscript, and quickly headed outside to play with your dog. When you came back inside, you immediately saw in your mother's eyes what a terrible decision it was to share your writing.

"I don't like these at all. I think you should burn them."

And you did burn most of them. But you didn't stop writing. You still haven't.

Your children have long accompanied you to your poetry readings and open mics. One night, you read one of your feistier poems, and your thirteen-year-old son asked, "Why is it that in your writing you're such a badass, but in real life you're so…different?"

Recently, you explained this to your partner. You tell him you realized at a young age you had to cut yourself in two, much like King Solomon had threatened with the baby claimed by two mothers. In this story, King Solomon was approached by two women, both of whom had just given birth. But one of the babies died. The mother who lost her child stole the other woman's infant. Both women claimed the infant as their own. King Solomon offered a solution: cut the baby in half and give one half to each mother. The mother whose child was dead agreed with his solution. But the other begged the king to hand the baby over to the other woman to spare the child's life. This was how the king revealed the identity of the infant's real mother.

For years, you pored over a children's book of Bible stories, and you were captivated by the most graphic, violent illustrations. The kind that struck fear and fascination in the mind of a curious child. The illustration accompanying this story of King Solomon in your children's book, showed a guard holding an infant by one leg, a sword up, ready to cut the child in half. Decades later, these images still haunt you. Just last night, you dreamt an infant was stolen from a man, and he was forced to watch a mob cut his child into pieces and eat his flesh.

You have written about your mother. You've written the stories she shared with you about her childhood in Colombia. You've turned her adolescent antics into near fairytales. You've marinated in her nostalgia—given a voice to her longing.

But recently, you've written a poetry chapbook titled, "The Mother Wound," where you expose the unhealed parts of yourself, places your mother left unprotected and unamended. This is all in sharp contrast to the poetry and short stories you wrote in your twenties, when you still believed in only one version of your mother. The one who saved the child. The selfless mother. You believed in the mother who woke up early to make breakfast, who held your hair out of your face when you were sick and vomiting, who said you were special—the "golden child." The one who said you were the only one who could make her laugh and smile on her darkest days. A "gift from God," she called you. Justifying your mother's transgressions was easy for you. In your mother's version of family life, your father was the villain. He brought her to the USA under the guise of a visit to meet his family and never took her back to Colombia.

According to your mother, she was essentially kidnapped by a white man twice her age. Taken from her family and homeland only to live in abject poverty, or *"en la ruina"* as she described it. The first home you remember was a 1960's Holiday Rambler, with an addition built onto it made of scrap wood and dumpster finds. In Barranquilla, your mother had servants. She wore silk dresses tailored to her petite build. She grew up without the burden of household chores and was married before learning to cook. Your mother often cried and talked about her country as if it were a phantom limb. When she finally visited her family after a twenty-year absence, she cried too. This wasn't the Colombia she remembered. In this new Colombia, she was easily lost.

Your mother elicited compassion and pity from you and your siblings. She relished in it. It was your job to console her when she cried and make her laugh during her most woeful moments. You became your mother's confidant, and as you grew up, you couldn't remember a time when you weren't your mother's panacea.

Your older sister, wise beyond her years, once told your mother, "It's not right. She's just a child."

"Fine! I won't have any friends at all then!" your mother yelled. Then of course, you were compelled to follow her, to hold her while she wept, to absorb her pain.

You tell your partner all these stories and you realize, there's another story to tell. You realize you can write your mother as a saint, or a monster. A tale of two mothers, and you are the infant held upside down by a guard, a sword threatening to cut you in half.

One mother made you believe you were special: the favorite, beloved. The other told you she was the only one you could trust, the one who told you your siblings hated you, kids from school hated you—only she could ever love you. One mother held you and sang songs to you, stroked your forehead and the bridge of your nose until you fell asleep. But the other mother sent your father into your bedroom when you woke from a nightmare, crying and screaming, and ordered him to beat you. One mother sent you a bouquet of red carnations on your sixteenth birthday, but the other let you believe those flowers were from a boy you'd loved for two years and laughed at you afterwards. One mother let you have a dog, but the other mother had your father dump that same dog in a field far away while you were at school because it had the audacity to bark. And she did this a dozen times, laughing every single time, laughing while you cried.

You haven't spoken to either mother in three years. She hasn't met her first grandson. She doesn't know you won a poetry contest or how you were just accepted into a PhD program. She doesn't know you finally found your person, and you're in love. She doesn't know you have nightmares about her, usually multiple times a week. The two mothers merge and separate over and over again.

Madre Santa
You wake up to the smell of your mother's weak coffee.

When you sit at the formica table, your mother greets you with a kiss and serves you your favorite: *migas*, and *cafe con leche*. Your mother prays before you eat. The *migas* are crunchy in all the right places, the oil-soaked corn tortillas leaving grease on your lips. The coffee turns nearly white from all the powdered creamer you pour into it. Your mother sings Spanish songs while she sweeps the floor, wearing a housecoat and rollers.

After breakfast, you both dress for the day. Your mother sprinkles her body with Avon talcum powder, while you dress yourself in a gingham sundress she sewed for you. You brush your hair, and she helps you place barrettes to keep it from falling over your face. You grab your book bag, armed with a Bible, *Despertad* and *Atalaya* magazines, pamphlets, and of course, your Book of Bible Stories.

When you leave the house, you beg your mom, "Please, can we go over the *lomita*?" Teens in low riders love to catch air going over the *lomita* at dangerous speeds. The *lomita*, a hill behind a local park, is your bit of excitement on the way to Bible studies and proselytizing. Your mother smiles, and nods. Both of you love to pretend you're in the Burt Reynolds movie, *Cannonball Run*. You think she's speeding over the hill, and you feel your stomach rise and drop as you squeal. Your mother laughs.

You talk to your mother the entire way to the first Bible study. Sometimes you hold her hand while she drives. She's a nervous driver. When she has to make a left turn, she says a little prayer, *"Jehovah Dios, ayudame!"* You feel her nerves, but you know God will help her with the left turn. Why wouldn't he? God must love her as much as you do.

When you get to the woman's house, she is young and meek and calls your mother *Dona*. Usually, your mother uses a red book about living forever to help women understand the Bible. But this woman is different: she can't read. Your mother takes out a slim book and you recognize it. It's how she taught you to read, in Spanish. You take out your own copy, with your name written on the cover. You're only five years old, and you read in Spanish fluently. But the young woman your mother is helping is still learning the letters, and the sounds they make. She stutters and struggles through each syllable of every word. It takes her several minutes to read one sentence. You feel impatient and read the following sentence as fast as possible. Pleased with yourself, you smile and look at your mother, but she is not smiling back.

When you get inside the car, your mother has a talk with you. She tells you what you did was wrong, that it humiliated the young woman. You immediately feel ashamed, even your heart blushes, and you cry easily.

Your mother makes you see when she says, "We are not here to shame people. Some adults can't read, and it is not their fault." She tells you she's not angry, she just wants you to have compassion for others. You nod, and you hug each other.

Back at home, your mother cooks white rice, topped with a runny egg, pears and milk blended together like a milkshake. Afterwards, she plays an album of classical music on her ancient and bulky record player. You know what this is, it's nap music. You always dread the thought of a nap, being alone in a dark room while your sister is still at school. But you're still small enough to hold, and your mother rocks you in her arms and sings, *"Nina bonita, nina bonita, duermate duermate nina bonita."* A couple of hours later, you wake up, your sister is back home, and *Gillighan's*

Island is playing on the TV set. Your mother makes you both peanut butter and jelly sandwiches with chocolate milk.

That evening, she gives you a bath and you add hot water whenever it cools too lukewarm. You love looking at your fingers, how they prune and turn wrinkly. You submerge yourself in water, until you can't hear a thing. It is the safest place you've ever been, besides your mother's arms.

Your mother brushes your hair and helps you put on your pajamas. After dinner, she stays in bed with you, holding your hand until you fall asleep.

Madre Monstro
You wake up to the smell of your mother's weak coffee.

You are no more than five years old and it's another sweltering hot summer day in the valley. While your mother is busy singing sad songs and washing dishes, you strip down to a pair of underwear and a white tank top and head outside. Outside is your favorite place. Outside with whatever dog you have at the time, and outside where the peach and pear trees shade you when you need relief. Outside, you lean back into your red Radio Flyer, feel the sun on your skin and close your eyes.

You're awakened abruptly by your mother, screaming at you and pulling at your arm. She says you are disgusting for going outside "like that." She says you must want perverted men to look at you. She spanks you again and again, to drive the point home. You bury your face on the rough and textured couch with the musty smell. You whisper, "I hate you. I hate you. I hate you," over and over again.

On Wednesday nights, you and your family attend Bible study at a single mother's house. Your father is the elder, the "conductor" of the study. You're still five years old, and your thighs stick to the plastic covered couches. The Bible study only lasts an hour, but to you, it feels like an entire summer. When the study is over, the woman's son, who had just graduated from high school, comes into the living room. He never joins the Bible study.

He touches your shoulder and opens the door to his bedroom. Across from you is your mother. You look back at her while she smiles and laughs with another woman, a "sister." You're waiting for her to hear the silent scream in your little body.

The son locks his bedroom door behind you and kneels, so you're face to face. He pushes you against the back of the door and begins to fondle you. Then, he kisses you, and you feel his warm tongue push between your lips and inside your mouth. You're frozen. He says nothing. He puts one finger to his lips, a sign to keep silent, to tell no one.

You return to the living room and see your mother sitting in the same place, still laughing. You go to her, pull on her, ask when you get to leave. She brushes you off, upset you interrupted her conversation. You're holding back tears. You feel stabbing pains in your stomach, and you think you might get sick.

When the study began, it was light outside. Now, it's getting darker, cooler. You're the last ones to leave out of a group of about twenty. The moment the car doors close, your father in the driver's seat and your mother in the passenger's. You speak up, breaking the forced oath of silence, "Nina's son kissed me on the lips. Like how grownups do in the movies. He put his tongue in my mouth."

Your father says nothing. He continues to put the car in reverse. But your mother says, offhandedly, "The next time he wants to do that to you, just tell him to ask us permission first."

When your mother puts you to bed, she kisses your forehead and says the usual prayer. After she leaves, you surround yourself with stuffed animals. You try to hug each one of them tight against your body all at once in your small, but fierce embrace. You cry and you beg God to forgive you.

That same summer, another teenage boy starts pulling down his pants, asking you to touch his "thing." You submit. It gets hard in your small hands. It makes you feel funny, but the boy is kind to you. He is pleased. But weeks later, while your mother and his mother are visiting, drinking Pepsi and eating slices of Wonder Bread, he asks if he can take you on a bike ride and both of your mothers' nod, barely pausing their conversation.

He sits you on the seat in front of him while he peddles. He sticks his hand in your shorts, and under your panties, and angrily demands, "Where is it? Where is it?" His fingers search for something, but you don't know what. Then you feel his fingers trying to pry you open, somewhere you've never sought out. Some place you didn't know existed. You squeal. You start to cry and ask to go home. Your mother calls his mother, and the father nearly beats the boy to death. Your voice, your words fueling the violence in his father's fists.

Your mother sends you back to that house, over and over again.

You're in the fifth grade and you hear about a talent show. All the kids are excited and talking about what they will do. You think of the piano organ in your room. You'd saved up your allowance for months, and when you saw it at a yard sale, you begged your parents for it and handed your money to the pretty blonde lady.

All day at school, you compose tunes inside your head. You dream up lyrics. You can't wait to get home and play your piano. You have no idea how to read music, but the organ came with some song books, and you start to teach yourself. But you find it's easier to move your fingers across the keys, until you find the sounds matching the music in your head. Then, you write the words in a notebook matching the sounds in your head and heart, and it feels like magic. It feels like you, the real you, emerging from a sad, quiet shell.

You tell your mother how you want to enter the talent show.

"You've never had lessons. We are too poor. You don't know how to play the piano. All the kids will laugh at you."

Months later you come home, and the piano organ is gone. You ask your mother, and she tells you she had your father throw it in the dump. She said it was for you, so you never embarrass yourself.

In the sixth grade, your aunt buys you a pretty journal, covered in blue and lavender fabric. You take it with you to school, and every chance you get, you write and you write. You write until you've written a seventy-page novella about two sisters, a rose garden, and a cruel mother. Your classmates notice, and by the end of the year, dozens of them have read your book.

In the eighth grade, you ask if you can borrow the electric typewriter your father bought for your mother that she never uses. You start to write another book. This one is called the *Poisonous Butterfly*. It too, is about two sisters, secrets, and even lust. You draw the cover, and the main character stands in the middle with long, wavy hair. You want her to look like Helena Bonham Carter, because you've become obsessed with the film *A Room With a View*; the one your mother says is a stupid, boring movie about a girl reading a book. But you don't care. You rent it every chance you get from the local video store. They know before you reach the counter what VHS you hold in your hands.

In the ninth grade you discover poetry. You buy your first ever book, one by E.E. Cummings. You love how he refuses to follow the rules of capitalization. As if no letter is more important than the other. You like how he breaks the rules, and you think lower case letters are prettier anyway. You also discover Anne Sexton, Sylvia Plath, and Emily Dickinson. You read a poem by Dickinson that will stay in your head for decades:

> *I'm nobody! Who are you?*
> *Are you nobody, too?*
> *Then there's a pair of us—don't tell!*
> *They'd banish us, you know*
>
> *How dreary to be somebody!*
> *How public, like a frog*
> *To tell your name the livelong day*
> *To an admiring bog!*

You spend your freshman year in solitude, eating lunch in the middle of the track field, writing poetry about the follies of religion, drawing pictures of sad, naked women. When you're writing or drawing, you are breathing. Not the automated breathing you do to survive. But the kind of breathing that only happens when you know you are doing what you should be doing. When you are on a certain path that feels right to you. Every breath is a promise to your authentic self.

When you make the mistake of sharing your book of poems with your mother, she tells you how much she dislikes your years' worth of work, and how you should burn it. Not only do you burn the poetry and the drawings, but also the novels, the *Poisonous Butterfly*, and the story about the rose garden and the two sisters written longhand in your beautiful journal.

For a while, you go without writing. You draw from time to time. But more than anything, you cut. You cut the inside of your arms, your thighs. You try to keep your hand over a flame. You sit in your closet, banging your head against the wall. You scream into pillows. After a while, even the cutting and burning no longer brings relief.

You decide to split yourself in two. You are the infant dangling from the guard's grip. But there is no mother to save you. No mother that lets you go, so you may live. So, you create another you, a false you. You go to the bathroom mirror and comb your hair differently. You practice a new smile, fake and garish. You call her Ashley. Ashley will be a good girl. The submissive one, the obedient daughter who will someday become the dutiful wife and mother, the one who will please her parents, her husband, and God.

Your mother isn't the only one alarmed by your poetry. Your words, your passions, your agonies, all in black and white, are called a red flag, a cause for concern. They say it reads like a suicide letter. So many goodbyes. Your English teacher reaches out to the counselor, who reaches out to your mother, and to your complete horror, she comes to your high school to meet with her.

"What did I do? What did I do to deserve this?"

Your mother cries, and howls, and never shuts up. The counselor spends the next hour trying to console her. She asks your mother questions. Were there signs? Had I been abused—physically, emotionally, sexually?

"No! Never!" your mother promises.

You sink back into your chair. You want out of your body. You look up at the fluorescent lights, listen to the hum of the electricity, and try to tune out her lies.

The school counselor refers your family to another therapist. He interviews your mother, and you hear her say the same things.

"Has she ever been sexually abused?"

"No, never!" she says.

This time you watch the yellow curtains in your therapist's office, how the slight wind through the screen window moves them, sucks them close, then releases them. You dream of release.

When you're seventeen, and in love with a boy who will become your husband, you sit your mother down. You tell her, "I remember everything." You ask her why. Why did she lie? She insists she was protecting you, protecting you from yourself, from your own memories. And weren't you grateful for her protection?

You dig your nails into your thighs. You grind your teeth. But then you forget, and you love her just as much as before.

You're engaged. You work full-time as a legal secretary, and in the little bit of time you have, you rush home and have lunch. Your mother tells you to make lunch for your fiancé and serve him before you sit down.

"You have to practice being a submissive, obedient wife," she says.

You're eighteen and you want to die. Your mother urges you to trick your husband and get pregnant. A child will keep you alive, she thinks.

You're twenty-five and you have two children. Also, you're divorced. You still want to die. In the hospital, your mother cries, "What did I ever do to deserve this?" Your hospital room is empty, except for your sister. But a crowd consoles your weeping mother. A gaggle of men and women put their arms around her and whisper, "There, there," as the tubes up your nose fill with charcoal.

Your children are grown, and you haven't tried to die in over a decade. You're getting your second master's degree.

Your mother says, "It's too hard for you. You should just be a hairdresser instead."

You pass all five tests to become a teacher on the first attempt. You call your mother.

"You passed because I prayed to Jehovah God, praise God!"

But you know it has nothing to do with God. You tell her so, and you hang up without saying goodbye.

You and your siblings try to protect your elderly mother from her favorite grandchild. The one who tried to kill her boyfriend, the one who stole from her, opened credit cards in her name, lied to her, used coke in her bathroom, abandoned her children for days. She chooses the granddaughter over the three of you. She changes her number. She tells your brother not to share it with you or your sisters.

Your mother fires her caregiver, who also tried to protect her. You talk to the caregiver on the phone, and you mention your job, your children. She says she didn't know you had any children. She didn't know you were a teacher, either.

"The only thing your mother ever said about you is that you couldn't keep a man."

You laugh. You tell her how much you love your job as an English teacher. You tell her about your children. You tell her about the book of stories you published. She asks you about school, and you share everything you know.

Months later, you see the caregiver on your college campus. She recognizes you from Facebook, hugs you, and she tells you, "Thank you." She says you're the reason she went back to school.

You. Wake. Up.

Your partner promises you, one day, you will have a piano. Not just a cheap keyboard, but a piano with all 88 keys.

"A baby grand!" he adds.

"But I don't even know how to play," you tell him.

"It doesn't matter…you deserve a piano," he reassures you.

And you imagine yourself, touching the keys, hoping it comes back to you, what found you so naturally and effortlessly as a child, but you already know it won't.

Maybe you are not the infant dangling upside down from the guard's grip. Maybe you only have one mother, and she is the infant, split into two: *Madre Santa, Madre Monstro.* Maybe you are the mother, the real mother, who let go, who sacrificed what was hers. Maybe that was a long time ago. And maybe now, you are the guard, cutting the tie that binds you.

Petrified Dog Shit

julia medina

I wrote it out like it was the perfect line someone more vicious, the antihero, perhaps, would revel in.

Fuck you.

He would roll in it like a dog and utterly salivate for its prick.

I was like the naïve high school girl convinced by the cunning older boy to sleep with him before he ships off to Europe, though he never does, and never loves her.

She never loved me, although I tried my best to force her heart to open just an inch and let me in. But in the end, I proved her right not to trust me all long.

She and I were both right in that sense—like the chicken and the egg. She would never love me, and I would give her good reason not to because I am the chicken, and she is hard boiled. Even more protective of herself now for the next lucky asshole. Sorry, you'll have to work a hell of a lot harder than I did to get to her soft golden center, where she'll look at you the way she so briefly looked at me.

It's not what happened, it's how I think about what happened.

What happened is, I loved someone but am incapable of loving.

No, she left me because I called her mean. Because we couldn't communicate with each other well.

That's still not it. I almost wish it was that. The truth is more embarrassing: she left me because I picked up a baggie at a bus stop and took a bump from it later that night, even after the fentanyl test came back inconclusive.

Circles, we went, about who said what and why. And in the end, I was the mean one.

She, the coward.

I, the bastard.

Feeding each other spools of harshness, evaporating the connection I thought was strong enough to withstand. How fucking wrong was I?

How fucking naïve.

You need to stop what you've been doing before you lose everything. She told me, smugly, like a threat.

Yeah, I should get fucking on that.

She's talking about the drinking. I remind her of her drunk dad. She's talking about making myself look like a jackass. It was so embarrassing to her. She's just trying to help me.

Fine. Whatever. I'll get sober again. If that's what will get her back, I'll do it.

But there's still the matter at hand. A Ziplock full of dead and decayed, ghost white magic mushrooms resembling tiny kneecap bones of an infant corpse.

Simply throwing them away is apparently not an option. Well, it should be, but I'm clearly incapable of doing that.

Do I ingest them? In my current state of mind?

I could do a lot worse. I could use a good ego death.

They look like dog shit that has been sitting in the grass for months, bleached white and stripped of nutrients by the sun. They taste sort of like how I imagine petrified dog shit tastes as well. Dry, but intensely chewy at the same time. Like vegan beef jerky. They keep getting stuck in my teeth. A lot of people can't stand the taste. Usually, I don't mind, but this strain of Psilocybin mushrooms is especially hard to stomach. They kind of look like something that was poisoned. In fact, it tastes like it too.

Why am I the kind of person who makes decisions like this?

I know some, but not too many people, who would snort white powder from a tiny dirty bag they found on the side-walk at a San Francisco bus stop. I grew up with a lot of idiots in high school doing too many shrooms. I know Larry. He did so much LSD, he had a three-month psychotic break where he thought he was in hell. Maybe that's what I need, a three-month break from reality.

If he ever truly taught me anything, it's to not do acid. He loves to spout his own hacky moral of that story: *know God and try to have a good time.* No, dude, it's that our family probably has a biological predisposition to schizophrenia, like how we have the alcoholic trait, and you found the key that unlocks it. I'm almost positive it has nothing to do with God.

Shrooms hit different. You don't see shit, you feel it. You think it. This sounds counterintuitive considering I pretty much have the emotional intelligence of a sea turtle, but it's much less terrifying to me than acid.

I bet Larry wouldn't last five seconds tripping on shrooms. Shrooms tell you the truth. Shrooms hold up the mirror so you can see inside your own soul. Imagine if he were to confront the part of him that causes people he is supposed to love, so much anguish. The part of him that caused my mother's depression, or my personality disorder, or his sons' narcissism. He would crumble.

He's not self-aware enough for shrooms.

He did acid and met the devil, and the devil tricked him into trying to see God, and he was punished by God, and sent to hell. He walked around for months, seeing nothing but death surrounding him. Then God approached him and said *how dare you try to see me with human eyes.* God offered my father the coward's way out: physical death.

God had punished him for having pride. For thinking he was such a supreme being, that he had the right to whatever he wants. Instead of realizing this about himself, he chose to still believe his desires are still supreme, and that it was a lesson in hedonism.

Then again, God isn't real, so it doesn't really matter.

Nothing really matters right now. I spent the day at Dolores Park with a friend, and she allowed me to tell the tale of how Brandy had broken my heart.

"Do you make all your friends listen to hour-long stories?" she asked.

The condensed version is this: I met Brandy at a mutual friend's birthday party. I sat at a picnic table at a bar I'd never been to across from this beautiful girl, who I'd heard about but hadn't met before. I felt something I hadn't felt since Liz, a palpable connection. I begged for her number, and called her that night, asking her if I could take her out. She rejected me.

I kept trying, like a fool. She always saw me as a jester, and she hated that about me. She wanted me to be more mature, more stable, more of anybody but myself. I thought she was amazing. She was getting her MBA in sustainable something or other. Lived in Berkeley and was beautiful, smart and had great taste in music: my kryptonite.

Just when I was about to give up on her, she gave a little slack and told me: *of course I like you,* because she couldn't deny the connection between us. It's more likely she said that to keep my attention squarely on her. It was never me she wanted—she made that clear. "My body doesn't know I don't want you," is one of the many confusing statements she made after the second time she'd dumped me. "You're sexy when you're stern," she said after upsetting me the very first time.

An entire eighth of shrooms is being digested inside my belly. They're making me nauseous, but I'm able to wash them all down with White Claws. Drink doesn't affect me on shrooms. I could drink it like water and not feel drunk.

I feel a quiet surrender-like calmness. Like how Larry recalled he was in a serene purple room when he was caught off guard by the Devil, who looked like Rudolph Valentino. The devil could lay right down in bed with me, and I would greet her warmly.

The first stage of shrooms, my favorite stage, is the euphoria. Complete nirvana. You can't help but feel your entire body smiling as it wells up inside you.

I'm watching the Simpsons in bed, waiting for the shrooms to take full effect. Mindlessly letting time go by. I only realize they are kicking into gear after I find myself unable to control my laughter. I don't know if I'd ever felt pure giddiness like this in my entire life. I imagine myself like a cartoon baby, with full rosy cheeks, giant eyelashes, and a wide, toothless smile, giggling at the tickling touch of a mother figure. Like the baby, I cannot control myself, the tickle in my stomach is too damn delightful.

I'm laughing so hard I'm wheezing. I'm laughing at the scene I'm watching, but it's not even funny. I just can't stop—every single line of dialog sends me into another fit of snorting and attempts to control my own volume. It's around 12am on a Saturday night. My roommate is on the other side of the wall, asleep. I know I must stop laughing somehow, so I turn off The Simpsons. The wait is over. The trip has begun.

I put on my giant, over-the-ear, noise-canceling headphones. This is my first-time tripping alone with my head full of music, and I'm not prepared for what happens next.

I get up to pee. My room is ten or so feet from the bathroom. I have no problem getting there. It's such a mundane, natural act I don't even think about it. It's when I finish peeing and attempt to stand up when the switch is flipped.

The song that's playing is a very intense, electronic, big bass-ey, one and when the chorus starts, the first big beat dropping, the walls around me start breathing in and out violently with the music. WHOMP. WHOMP. WHOMP-WHOMPWHOMP. WHOMP. WHOMP. Like I'm getting thrashed around by the music, my body is unstable on two feet. I hold on to the wall, attempting to steady myself, but it keeps moving in strong waves orchestrated by the melody. I look in the mirror to see if the world is really morphing around me, and I have to look away, because it looks like my face is made of clay, and it's being molded and squished by invisible hands. Holy fuck, this is intense. I'm in a fishbowl. Someone is shaking my habitat—nothing will stand still. I realize I probably can't walk the ten feet back to my room on my own two legs without flailing all over the place, so I decide it's better to crawl instead. On my hands and knees, I attempt to focus on just getting back to my room, but it feels like a mile away. I wonder if my roommate can hear me. I wonder if I can make it back without disturbing him.

It's difficult, but being on all fours makes me barely steady enough to not run into walls. I'm on a tightrope, and I can't keep my balance to save my life. Thank God I'm crawling because I, without a doubt, would be crashing into these walls. It's like that earthquake ride at Universal Studios. The ground is entirely volatile, and I'm not strapped into my seat.

I make it safely to my room. Still on all fours, but I'm relieved when I can quietly close the door behind me.

Here I am, safe.

Nobody in the world knows this is happening.

This is real, this *is* happening, but only I'm experiencing it, and that feels profound.

The world is asleep right now. I'm alone. The walls look like they are made of Jell-O, they're dancing to the music even though they can't hear it. I'm the only one who can hear this music. How does the wall know how to dance to its rhythm?

For a long time, I just stay there, on all fours, unable to do anything but that. My thoughts are going a thousand miles a minute. *This is fucking crazy. This is fucking intense. Nobody else even knows what is happening to me. I'm in fucking trouble. I can't stand up. I can't think straight. I need to remember what is happening. I need to remember what this feels like because it's absolutely fucking bonkers.*

It occurs to me that I should record myself on video. If I record myself, I will be able to remember this more clearly later. I want to be able to look back, and maybe it will capture some of the insanity going on around me right now.

I press record and turn the screen off because I'm scared to look at myself after what just happened in the bathroom. For a long while, I just lay on my belly, holding myself up by my forearms, and let my mind take me away. *I have to remember this feeling. It's like I'm a fucking infant. I can't stand up. My brain isn't sending the correct signals to make my limbs move the way I want them too. What if this doesn't go away? What if I don't remember?* I urge myself to find a notebook. *I need to remember.* I take a pen. *I need to remember.* I put the pen to the paper, but I can't hold the pen normally. My fingers can't remember how the pen is supposed to be held between the thumb and index finger, then be supported by the middle finger, all three working together to cradle the pen. Instead, I have to hold it like a dagger, like I'm trying to carve hieroglyphics onto a stone slab. It takes me minutes to write the four simple words. Why can't I use the goddamn pen?

I keep getting distracted by the hilarity of not being able to hold a pen. Fits of laughter, that last for what feels like forever.

I finally finished the note.

I NEED TO REMEMBER.

I hold it up to my computer, like I'm a hostage and am sending my message to the world. I wonder if someone who works for Zoom is going to see me on video like this, holding up this fucking sign, like a cry for help and send authorities to my location.

I'm trying to write something else for the camera. I want it to know that I'm aware of the quiet outside of my head. But it's difficult. Something is still blocking my brain from telling my hand what to write, how to spell, how to put words in a cohesive order. It comes out like nonsense, but I feel satisfied the message is out there.

I AM ACUTELY AWARE OF THE QUIET is what I intend, but again, it's gibberish on the page.

When Larry had his psychotic break, his motor functions still worked. He was trapped in a world that scared him, but he could still write letters, I imagine. I can't even fucking stand.

What if I never go back to normal? What if I just permanently fucked myself? I feel like a goddamn vegetable. My heart is racing as these things occur to me. *What the fuck did I do?* What if I never get my mind back? What if I stay like this? I'll be locked up at Napa state. They'll say: *she was perfectly of sound mind before she ate too many shrooms one night.* And they'll study me and learn about the effects of psychedelics on the brain.

That, or I'm going to fucking die.

I would rather die than live like this.

Where is God to give me my option, like he did for Larry?

I'm convinced this will end in one of these two ways. But on the off chance that neither happen, I have to fucking remember.

I have to be better. I have to do better if I make it out alive. I have to do better than he did.

Alexandra Bergmann is a writer, educator, and scientist from the San Francisco Bay Area. They hold an MFA from the Iowa Writers' Workshop. Her poems have appeared in *The Madison Review*, *Tendon*, *SEISMA Magazine*, and elsewhere.

Ian Day is a writer living in Southern California. He has a degree in Creative Writing from Central Washington University. This is his first publication.

Merridawn Duckler is a writer and visual artist, author of INTERSTATE (dancing girl press) IDIOM (Harbor Review) MISSPENT YOUTH (rinky dink press) and ARRANGEMENT (Southernmost Books.) Winner of the Beulah Rose poetry prize from Smartish Pace, the Elizabeth Sloane Tyler Memorial Award Woven Tale Press, judged by Ann Beattie and the Drama prize from Arts and Letters at Georgia College. Work in Best Small Fictions 2025.

Cecilia Januszewski is a recent graduate and the proud holder of a BA in linguistic anthropology; perhaps the most interesting, least marketable degree. She lives in Portland, Oregon, where she spends her free time going on long walks, sneaking into literature courses, and drafting her first novel. She has been previously published in *Blue Marble Review*, *Manuscripts*, *Quibble*, and *Quabbin Quills*, where she is now an editorial board member.

Joshua Kepfer lives in California where he enjoys exploring the wilderness of the mountains and ocean with his wife and daughter. Much of his inspiration to write prose, music, and poetry comes from nature and his faith in Jesus. He has work published in *Stories and Symmetries, Merganser Magazine, Azure Journal, Peregrine Journal, IHRAM,* and more.

Elina Kumra is a short fiction and poetry writer from the Bay Area.

Bee Lazar (they/them), aka "Beaks" to many, is a self-acclaimed professional dog walker and avid collage enthusiast. Dig up their work in *Reed Magazine, The Lupa Newsletter, Tension Literary, EcoTheo Review,* and upcoming in *A Brand New Word* in the *End Drops Out,* an anthology under *West Trade Review.*

Lance Mazmanian appears in *London Writers' Salon, Fiction on the Web UK, Poetries in English Magazine* (Los Angeles), more. RPG legend David Hargrave (RIP), origin of Arduin, created Mazmanian's elaborate grave "Lancer's Rest" scheduled for 2026.

Julia Medina (she/her) is a queer essayist from San Francisco. She received her MFA in Creative Nonfiction from the University of San Francisco and has been published in university presses: *The Four Leaf Collective* and *The Ignatian.* She is currently working on her first essay collection, *Bad Idea Machine.*

Laine Perry grew up in Northern California, and later, Mercer Island, WA. She studied play writing under Gladden Schrock, at Bennington College in Vermont. Shortly thereafter she began working in the film industry in the art department on independent films and music videos. Laine has written many short stories and has written, produced and directed two films. She currently lives in the Northwest, where she is at work on her first novel.

JoAnna Scandiffio am a graduate gemologist living in San Francisco. My poems are like bird nests, made with fragments randomly connected to hold the moment. My work has appeared in *Calyx, The Poeming Pigeon, The MacGuffin, Italian Americana, The RavensPerch* and other journals, I am a Pushcart Prize Nominee. My chapbook water is never still will be forthcoming from *Finishing Line Press*.

Shobha Tharoor Srinivasan is an award-winning author and voice-over artist whose work spans fiction, nonfiction, and children's literature. Winner of the 68th National Film Award for Best Narration (India, 2022), her books—published in India and the USA—include *It's Time to Rhyme, Prince with a Paintbrush,* and *Good Innings.* Her poems and stories explore themes ranging from the environment to idiomatic expressions and have been widely recognized, anthologized, and adapted. Shobha is also a frequent speaker and literary festival panelist.

Nicholas Viglietti is a writer from Sacramento, CA. He built homes on the gulf coast for two years after Katrina. Up in Mon-tucky, he cut trails in the wilderness. He pedaled from Sac-town to S.D. He's a seventh-life party-hack, attempting to rip chill lines in the madness.

Kristy Webster is the daughter of a Colombian immigrant and a Montana cowboy. She is the author of *The Gift of an Imaginary Girl: Coco and Other Stories* published by *A Word with You Press* (2015) and *Heretic: a story of spiritual liberation in poems*, published by *Beyond the Veil Press* (2022). She earned her MFA in Creative Writing from Pacific Lutheran University and a Master's in Teaching from Heritage University. She works as a full-time English instructor at Yakima Valley College, Grandview campus, Washington state.

Lenore Weiss lives in Oakland, California and is a member of the San Francisco Writers Grotto. She also serves as the Associate Creative Nonfiction (CNF) Editor for the Mud Season Review. Her novel *Pulp into Paper* was published last year as was a new poetry collection, *Video Game Pointers*. Prior poetry collections form a trilogy about love, loss, and being mortal: *Cutting Down the Last Tree on Easter Island* (West End Press, 2012), *Two Places* (Kelsay Books, 2014), and *The Golem* (Hakodesh Word Press, 2017).

Evan Morgan Williams is the recipient of a 2024 Oregon Literary Fellowship. He is the author of four collections of stories: *Thorn* (BkMk Press, 2014), *Canyons* (2018), *Stories of the New West* (Main Street Rag Press, 2021), and *The Divide* (forthcoming, Cornerstone Press, 2026). Williams' work has appeared in *Kenyon Review, Witness, Zyzzyva*, and *Alaska Quarterly Review*. He holds an MFA, tattered and faded, from the University of Montana (1991).